An Unlikely Amish Match

Vannetta Chapman

LOVE INSPIRED

INSPIRATIONAL ROMANCE

Recycling programs for this product may not exist in your area.

ISBN-13: 978-1-335-48793-3

An Unlikely Amish Match

Copyright © 2020 by Vannetta Chapman

This edition published by arrangement with Harlequin Books S.A.

For questions and comments about the quality of this book, please contact us at CustomerService@Harlequin.com.

Love Inspired
22 Adelaide St. West, 40th Floor
Toronto, Ontario M5H 4E3, Canada
www.Harlequin.com

Printed in U.S.A.

"Oh, so you think that's funny. Is that why you're laughing?"

Micah wasn't interested in Susannah, and she certainly wasn't interested in him—not that way. They were just hanging out together, helping him through a tough time until he was able to return home.

She'd do well to keep that thought front and center.

When he returned and presented her with the shoe, she grabbed it from him with a curt "I'm going to get even for this."

But his response was a mere whisper that sent goose bumps down her arms. "You look awfully pretty in the moonlight, Susannah Beiler."

Which set off every emotional alarm she possessed.

Was he flirting with her?

What was she doing standing in the moonlight with Micah Fisher? She was supposed to be keeping an eye on him—keeping him out of trouble.

Micah said, "Let me gather up our stuff. Then we can walk back by the road. It'll give our clothes time to dry off a bit."

But a small part of her wished the night could go on and on...

Vannetta Chapman has published over one hundred articles in Christian family magazines and received over two dozen awards from Romance Writers of America chapter groups. She discovered her love for the Amish while researching her grandfather's birthplace of Albion, Pennsylvania. Her first novel, *A Simple Amish Christmas*, quickly became a bestseller. Chapman lives in Texas Hill Country with her husband.

Books by Vannetta Chapman

Love Inspired

Indiana Amish Brides

A Widow's Hope
Amish Christmas Memories
A Perfect Amish Match
The Amish Christmas Matchmaker
An Unlikely Amish Match

Visit the Author Profile page at Harlequin.com.

Being confident of this very thing, that he which hath begun a good work in you will perform it until the day of Jesus Christ.
—*Philippians* 1:6

But when he was yet a great way off, his father saw him, and had compassion, and ran, and fell on his neck, and kissed him.
—*Luke* 15:20

This book is dedicated to Ms. Peggy Looper,
who inspired in me a real love
for the art of storytelling.

Chapter One

Susannah Beiler was carrying a to-go bag holding half of a cinnamon roll in one hand and her coffee in the other when she stepped out of Cabin Coffee and started across the street. At that exact moment, a large Ford pickup truck careened to the curb. Her friend Deborah pulled her back with a laugh and a smile. "Wouldn't do to have you flattened on the streets of Goshen on this beautiful spring day."

After all she'd been through the last two years, it would be ironic. Susannah shook off that thought and would have walked across the street that was now clear, but Deborah stepped back under the canopy of the coffee shop and nodded toward the truck. "Do you ever wonder why people act like that?"

The music was blaring at such a high level that the vehicle was practically rocking. The truck sported a bright blue paint job with streaks of lightning painted down the side, a large chrome bumper and spinning tire rims.

"Why would you jack it up so high?" Susannah crossed her arms, tapping her right index finger against her left arm. Sometimes she felt like she didn't understand other people at all.

"And who would want to purchase such big tires? They look as if they'd fit a tractor."

"*Ya*, I'm not sure what the point is."

They glanced at one another when a young man jumped out of the truck, empty fast-food bags and soda cans trailing after him. He noticed the girls, smiled in a cocky *Englisch* way and then realized they were staring at the litter that had escaped from the truck.

"Oops." He snatched up the trash and tossed it into an adjacent trash can before once again flashing them both a smile.

He was a bit taller than Susannah, but then, most men were. He was also built like the mule her *dat* kept to watch over the goats—stocky and muscular. Blue jeans, a T-shirt that sported the logo of some rock and roll band, and sandy-colored hair flopping into his eyes and curling at his neck completed the picture.

Deborah laughed, but Susannah shook her head.

She couldn't abide rude people, and this guy seemed oblivious that the truck was obnoxious and the music was too loud.

The driver of the truck had put the vehicle into Park and jumped out. He had bright red hair sticking out from his ball cap, but other than that he could have been a twin to the first guy. As Susannah and Deborah watched, he walked up to his buddy, and they performed some complicated handshake.

"Take care, man."

"You know it." The first guy reached into the truck and snatched out a ball cap and a faded backpack.

"Later."

"Much."

The driver hopped back into the truck and sped away. The sandy-haired guy winked at Susannah and Deborah, pulled a cell phone out of his pocket and proceeded to stare at it as he walked in the opposite direction.

"Clueless," Susannah said, rubbing at the brow over her right eye. "He'll be lucky if he doesn't fall off the sidewalk the way he's staring down at that phone."

"Maybe."

"Are you kidding me?"

"I'm only saying that just because he's different doesn't mean that he's bad."

"I didn't say he was bad."

"Uh-huh, but the look you gave the both of them would have frightened a small child."

"Really?"

"Definitely. You've always been able to do that—stop someone in their tracks." Deborah linked their arms together and turned them toward her buggy. "Are you sure you don't want to be a teacher?"

"I'm not sure of much, but I am sure of that."

"Which is just as well, because you're a fabulous quilter."

"Danki."

"Off we go to the fabric store, then."

Which cheered up Susannah immensely. Even if she didn't purchase anything, being around bolts of fabric had a way of encouraging her on the darkest of days. During the worst of her chemotherapy treatments, she'd often stopped into the local fabric store simply to enjoy the smell and touch of new fabric. When she was too sick to piece or quilt, she'd sometimes sit with a basketful of different-colored cotton swatches, dreaming of what she would sew as soon as she was better.

There was something about brushing her fingertips over the cotton, envisioning the pattern she would use and the quilts she would make and picturing the smiles on tourists who purchased them. Quilting was her way of spreading joy, and wasn't that what a person of faith was supposed to do?

Deborah was describing her *dat* having to battle his way through a thicket of thorny brush to free a goat that had managed to become ensnared. The goat had taken one look at Deborah's *dat* and scampered off in the opposite direction, leaving him wondering why he'd thought he needed to save the animal in the first place. "'Goats are resourceful animals, Deborah. Never forget it,'" Deborah finished with a spot-on imitation of her *dat*. She always could tell a good story, and they were both laughing by the time they reached the fabric store.

Susannah enjoyed the rest of the afternoon.

She forgot all about the *Englischer*.

And she arrived home humming a tune and feeling immeasurably better than she had when she had awakened that morning. Some days she still woke terrified that the cancer had returned, certain that she was about to be plunged back into the cycle of doctor's visits and tests and treatments. Some days were still harder than others.

But her day had improved, and her mood had lightened with it.

"Mind fetching the mail for me?" Her *mamm* had been up since before sunrise—they both had. While Susannah did her best to help with household chores, her *mamm* often shooed her away, telling her to go rest or step outside for a while or spend an hour in her quilting room.

At the moment, her *mamm*'s apron was a mess, her hair was escaping from her *kapp* and her hands were covered in bread dough. Two loaves were already baking in the oven and two she'd finished kneading sat on the counter.

Sometimes Susannah wondered why they still made the bread from scratch, since loaves were certainly cheaper to purchase at the grocery store. She did love the smell of fresh-baked bread, though.

"And please take your *schweschdern*. They're full of energy today."

Sharon and Shiloh dropped the dolls they were playing with and ran toward the front door.

"Sweaters first," Susannah said. Though it was the last week of April, the afternoons cooled quickly. The twins reversed directions and ran for their cubbies. When the girls were born, her *dat* had placed cubbies in the mudroom with their names marked at a level they could now easily read.

"They sound more like puppies on the loose than children," Susannah said.

She adored her little *schweschdern*. Her *mamm* had been twenty when Susannah was born and forty when the twins came along. They were the siblings she never thought she'd have, and she prayed every day that they hadn't inherited the gene that had caused her ovarian cancer. She didn't want anyone else to have to endure such a thing, especially not her *schweschdern*.

"Like I said—full of energy. I wouldn't mind if you stayed out with them a half hour or so, give them time to run some of it off."

Susannah thought her mother was one of the most hardworking women she knew, but twin five-year-olds could wear anyone down.

"Finish that bread and then sit down with a cup of tea. I have a feeling you've earned it today."

The twins catapulted back into the kitchen.

"I'm ready." Shiloh reached for her hand.

"Me, too. I wonder if we have a letter from *Mammi*." Sharon dashed to the front door.

"Don't run too far ahead," Susannah called out.

The girls looked identical—white-blond hair, blue eyes and a thin build. The only physical difference that was easy to spot was that Sharon had freckles and Shiloh didn't. Their personalities were quite opposite. Sharon was always running ahead—energetic, enthusiastic and fearless. Shiloh preferred to hang back and carefully watch. She also liked holding hands, while Sharon proclaimed that was for babies.

By the time Susannah and Shiloh descended the front porch steps, Sharon was already waiting at the lane— hands on her hips, a scowl on her face and a whine in her voice. "Why are you so slow? Come on already."

The day was one of those glorious spring days that Susannah often daydreamed about in the winter. The leaves were a green so bright they caused you to blink, and the flowers planted earlier that month had burst into a rainbow of color. The sky was blue, the sun shone brightly and the weather was cool enough to require a sweater but without a cold north breeze.

Perfect.

They picked wildflowers as they rambled down the lane.

Both girls stooped to watch ants carrying tiny pieces of grass.

And they fed carrots to Percy, their buggy horse, who was grazing in the field that ran alongside the lane.

Susannah's mind called up all the things she had to

be thankful for—her family, her health, a community that had supported her through a difficult time and now a perfect spring afternoon.

Ten minutes later, they reached the mailbox. Susannah had her hand inside, trying to reach to the back, where it seemed at least one piece of mail always managed to land, when Shiloh stepped closer and Sharon began to bounce from foot to foot.

"Someone's coming," Sharon said.

Susannah shielded her eyes against the afternoon sun, at first curious and then disbelieving and finally completely confused. What was *he* doing here?

Micah Fisher had taken his time finding his way out to the farm. He'd figured that as long as he was in town, he might as well check things out. Then he'd realized he was hungry again, so he'd stopped by the coffee shop where the two Amish ladies had been standing. He ate a leisurely lunch and used the time to charge his phone since he wouldn't be able to do so at his grandparents' farm.

The sun was low in the western sky by the time he hitched a ride to the edge of town. The driver let him out at a dirt road that led to several Amish farms. He'd never been to visit his grandparents before. They always came to Maine. But he had no trouble finding their place. His *mamm*'s instructions had been very clear.

As he drew close to the lane that led to the farmhouse, he noticed a young woman standing by the mailbox. A little girl was holding her hand and another was hopping from foot to foot. They were all three staring at him.

"Howdy," he said.

The woman only nodded, but the two girls responded with "Hello"—one whispered and the other shouted.

"Can we help you?" the woman asked. "Are you… lost?"

"*Nein.* At least I don't think I am."

"You must be if you're here. This is the end of the road."

Micah pointed to the farm next door. "Abigail and John Fisher live there?"

"They do."

"Then I'm not lost." He snatched off his baseball cap, rubbed his hand over the top of his head and then yanked the cap back on and down to shield his eyes. "Say, don't I know you?"

"Absolutely not."

"But I've seen you before…in town, when I first arrived. You were standing outside the bakery with a plain-looking girl."

"If you mean Amish, we all are."

"No, I meant plain." He smiled to suggest he was teasing, though honestly the other girl had been so pale as to be translucent and had worn the traditional white *kapp* and a gray dress. She could have been a cloud or a puff of fog or a figment of his imagination.

But the girl in front of him?

She wasn't someone you'd quickly forget—daring brown eyes, a *kapp* pulled so tightly that not a hair escaped, which only served to accentuate the exquisite shape of her eyes, bright color in her cheeks and a sweet curve to her lips. Her dress was a pretty dark green with a matching apron.

And she was his neighbor?

Perhaps *Gotte* had provided him an ally through this trying time of his life.

Micah stepped forward and held out his hand. "I'm Micah—Micah Fisher. Pleased to meet you."

"You're not *Englisch*?" Instead of shaking his hand, she reached for her other sister. They had to be siblings from the way they looked up at her and waited to see what she'd do next.

"Of course I'm not."

"So you're Amish?" She stared pointedly at his clothing—tennis shoes, blue jeans, T-shirt and ball cap. Pretty much what he wore every day.

"I'm as Plain and simple as they come."

"I somehow doubt that."

"Since we're going to be neighbors, I suppose I should know your name."

"Neighbors?"

"*Ya*. I've come to live with my *daddi* and *mammi*—at least for a few months. My parents think it will straighten me out." He tugged his ball cap lower and peered down the lane. "I thought the bishop lived next door."

"He does."

"Oh. You're the bishop's *dochder*?"

"We all are," the little girl with freckles cried. "I'm Sharon and that's Shiloh and that is Susannah."

"Nice to meet you, Sharon and Shiloh and Susannah."

Sharon lost interest and squatted to pick up some of the rocks lining the caliche lane. Shiloh hid behind her *schweschder*'s skirt, and Susannah scowled at him.

So, not an ally.

"I knew the bishop lived next door, but no one told me he had such pretty *doschdern*."

Susannah's eyes widened even more, but it was Shiloh who peeked out from behind her skirt and said, "He just called you pretty."

"Actually, I called you all pretty."

Shiloh ducked back behind Susannah.

Susannah narrowed her eyes as if she was squinting into the sun, only she wasn't. "Do you talk to every girl you meet that way?"

"Not all of them—no."

"And do you always dress like that?"

"What's wrong with how I'm dressed?"

"And why did you arrive in a pickup truck?"

"Because a friend offered to bring me."

"An *Englisch* friend?"

"Say, what is this—the third degree? It feels like it, and as far as I know, I've done nothing to land me in trouble."

"Yet." Susannah snatched up Sharon's hand and turned back toward the bishop's house.

"It was *gut* to meet you," he called out, knowing it would fluster her. Just his luck that the girl next door would be a killjoy. He'd met enough Amish girls like her to fill the back of a pickup truck twice over.

They were so disapproving.

It rankled him.

It also made him want to do something reckless, like throw a party or take off for points unknown or walk back to town and see a movie. But he didn't do any of those things. He didn't know anyone to invite to a party—yet. All of Goshen was unknown, and he wasn't even sure they had a movie house. Plus, he had no money to pay for a movie.

He sighed heavily, considering what lay before him. He'd promised his parents that he would come to Goshen and stay for at least six months. He realized he might as well walk up to the farmhouse. There was no point in avoiding it, but first he pulled out his phone, tapped the Snapchat button and held the phone up in front of him.

"I've arrived at the far reaches of northern Indiana. Let's hope I can survive life on the farm." He made what he hoped was a hilarious face, added a filter and frame, and then clicked the post button. Sticking the phone into his back pocket, he trudged down the lane toward his grandparents' house and what was probably going to be the longest six months of his life.

Susannah wasn't going to bring up the subject of their new neighbor to her parents. She actually was trying to forget him. She liked her life exactly as it was. The last thing she needed was trouble living next door, and Micah Fisher definitely looked like trouble.

They'd paused to bless the food and had just begun passing around the dishes of ham casserole, fresh bread, carrots and salad when Sharon starting chatting away about their encounter with Micah.

"He's tall and he talks funny."

"He wears a crazy hat," Shiloh added.

"And he wanted to shake Susannah's hand, but she didn't want to."

"And he said we were pretty—he said we were *all* pretty." Shiloh pulled in her bottom lip as she concentrated on cutting up her ham into small bites.

Her *dat* helped Sharon to scoop a spoonful of carrots onto her plate. "John mentioned to me that the boy was coming to stay with them for a while."

"He hardly seems like a boy." Susannah felt a slow blush creep up her neck when both her parents turned to stare at her. "What I mean is that he seemed to act like a *youngie*, though plainly he was older—I'd guess around twenty."

She could tell that her explanation hadn't cleared up anything, so she backed up and told them of seeing him in town, of the truck and the trash and the *Englisch* clothes. She didn't bring up the cell phone. That felt like tattling. No doubt his grandparents, and her *dat*, would know about it soon enough.

"Not everyone is as settled as you are, dear. I believe *Gotte* used your illness to mature you." Her *mamm* buttered a piece of bread—hot, fresh and savory. Perhaps homemade was better.

"And hopefully to make you even more compassionate toward others." Her *dat*'s smile softened his words. "No doubt Micah is trying to find his way as many of our youth are—though, as you say, he's hardly a *youngie* anymore. Just turned twenty-five, if I remember correctly from what John said."

"The same as you." Her mother looked pleased, as if sharing the same age would make them best pals.

Susannah didn't think that was likely.

Her life had finally settled down. She had no desire to complicate it with the likes of Micah.

The rest of the meal passed in a flurry of conversation. Sharon chattered on about the kittens in the barn and how she was planning to name each one. Shiloh had read another of the picture books from the library, and she insisted on describing it in great detail. Her *mamm* reminded Susannah that church would be at the Kings' on Sunday, and that they had agreed to go over and help Mose prepare on Saturday. And her *dat* described a young mare that had been brought in for shoeing. "Four white socks and a patch on her forehead—pretty thing."

Susannah heard the conversations going on around her, but her mind kept volleying between the log-cabin quilt she'd started the day before and the new neighbor next door.

She didn't want a new neighbor.

Why couldn't things stay as they were?

She couldn't have explained what made her think so, but somehow she was certain that the comfortable rhythm of their days was about to change.

And then, as if to confirm her thoughts, her *dat* said, "Oh, I forgot to mention that Micah is going to be working in my shop a couple hours each afternoon. Perhaps we can have him over for dinner sometime."

The smile on her *mamm*'s face told Susannah there was no use arguing with that.

Well, she'd just have to endure Micah's presence though she did not and would not approve of his *Englisch* ways.

Her *dat* had said he was staying awhile.

Micah had mentioned a few months.

Surely it couldn't be for a terribly long time. He wasn't moving in, and he hadn't been carrying any luggage, just the denim backpack. With any luck, he'd be gone by the first day of summer.

As was his habit, her *dat* took the twins out with him to do a final check of the animals. Susannah and her mother were cleaning the dishes when the conversation returned to Micah.

"Do you think you might like him?"

"Oh, I'm pretty sure we're polar opposites."

"Not always a bad thing."

"It's not going to happen, *Mamm*." The words came out more harshly than she'd intended. "We've spoken of this. I don't believe… That is, I'm sure what you're thinking of isn't *Gotte*'s plan for me."

"You mean marrying."

"*Ya*. I mean marrying."

"Because of your cancer—which is gone."

"Gone, yes, but it could come back, and more than that, the whole experience has left me changed."

"In more ways than one." Her *mamm* turned to study her though her hands remained in the sudsy water. "You've turned into a fine young woman, Susannah— a godly woman."

"You're changing the subject. Any man—any Amish man—would want a houseful of children." Susannah refused to meet her mother's gaze. Instead, she focused on the plate she was drying.

"Just because Samuel felt that way doesn't mean every man feels the same."

"We both know that Samuel and I were…mismatched. His breaking up with me, it was hard, but I felt immediately better once it was done."

"But…"

"But I learned, *Mamm*. I learned that men have certain expectations from marriage."

Why was it that speaking of this always brought tears to her eyes? She'd grown accustomed to the facts—to the limitations—of her life, but it seemed as if a certain part of her heart remained bruised. "How does the proverb go? 'No woman can be happy with less than seven to cook for'? I suspect no Amish man can be happy with less than seven to provide for."

"Children come to us in different ways."

"You're speaking of adoption—which is rare in an Amish community."

"Rare but not unheard-of." Her *mamm* wiped her hands on a dish towel, reached out and put a hand on each of Susannah's shoulders, turning her toward her.

Susannah couldn't resist the need to look up, to look into her *mamm*'s eyes and face her dreams and fears head-on.

"I'm only saying that you shouldn't assume you know *Gotte*'s plan for your life. Our ways are not *Gotte*'s ways, and that's something to be grateful for."

Once Susannah nodded that she understood, her *mamm* picked up another dish and slipped it into the dishwater. Susannah swiped at the tears that had slipped down her cheeks, feeling foolish and wishing she could keep a better rein on her emotions.

Her melancholy wasn't about Micah. It was about her parents' expectations for her life. Micah, she felt nothing except pity for—and perhaps a tad of irritation.

"Just wait until you meet Micah, then you'll understand."

"Will I, now?"

"I'm more likely to marry Widower King."

"Who is a fine man and a *gut* addition to our community."

"And he's thirty-five years old."

"Is he, now?"

They shared a smile. Her *mamm* knew very well how old Mose King was and that Susannah didn't have an ounce of romantic feelings for the man.

"You wouldn't have to worry about not being able to have children," her *mamm* joked.

"Indeed—six would be plenty, especially when those six are three pairs of twins."

"And all boys."

"All of them *full of energy*." Susannah purposely used her mother's words from earlier that afternoon.

They finished cleaning up the kitchen and walked onto the front porch to watch for her *dat* and the twins.

"I understand your not being interested in Micah, though you'd do well to remember that our first impression of someone isn't always the best."

"Fair enough."

"There's something else you should know, though."

Susannah sank into the rocker beside her *mamm*. She thought that twilight might be her favorite time of day. Something in her soul felt soothed by watching the sun set across their fields and her *dat* walking hand in hand with the twins toward the house.

"Micah's parents have been corresponding with Abigail and John. When it was decided he would move here, they shared the letter with both me and your *dat*. He's had a bit of a hard time, which is why he's here."

"Okay." She said the word slowly, tempted to add an *I thought so*.

"What I'm saying is that Micah will be here for at least six months—"

"Six months?" Susannah realized her mouth was hanging open and snapped it shut.

"And he'll be here helping your *dat* every day, so it could be that *Gotte* has put him in our path for a special reason."

Susannah stifled a groan.

"There's a real possibility that what Micah needs most is not a girlfriend but simply a friend, and that's something that we can each be."

Chapter Two

Micah's first night with his grandparents went fairly well. It was the next morning that things took an unpleasant turn, when they laid down the law, so to speak.

His *dat*'s parents were in their midsixties—not too old to farm, but old enough that they should be slowing down. That wasn't happening. His *daddi*, John Fisher, was built like an ox. Micah's mother had always said that Micah inherited his size from the man, but Micah didn't see it. He was as muscular as the next guy, but his grandfather's forearm look like corded rope. *Forearm*—singular. He'd lost his right arm in a harvesting accident when he was just twenty years old. It had made him tough and intolerant of weakness of any type.

He was also a very serious man. Micah couldn't imagine that they'd come from the same gene pool.

Abigail Fisher was stern as well, but with a soft spot for her grandchildren. Growing up in Maine, Micah had seen his *mammi*'s letters arrive weekly. They always contained a paragraph addressed to each of the eight children. Her Christmas presents were always mailed well before Christmas Day—practical items, lovingly made.

And his *mammi* and *daddi* visited occasionally, though certainly not every year.

In truth, Micah felt as if he hardly knew his grandparents, and though he loved them as he thought grandchildren should, he didn't think they had much in common. In fact, from the expression on his *daddi*'s face he wasn't sure the man really wanted him there. So why had he agreed to this ridiculous plan? How was Micah supposed to become a different person—*a more mature person* in the words of his *dat*—by living in a different state for six months?

Daddi didn't look up until they'd finished eating. Then he cradled his coffee mug in his left hand and waited until he was sure he had Micah's attention. "We expect you to work every day."

"Okay. That's fair." Micah brushed his hair away from his eyes and sat up straighter. "I can start looking for something today."

"No need to do that. I have it all arranged."

"All arranged?"

"To begin with, you'll be expected to carry your share of the work around here—the same as any grown man. I realize that will be different from what you're used to back home. I'm aware that your parents have coddled you."

Micah frowned at the last biscuit on his plate and focused on not saying the response that immediately came to mind. His thoughts scrambled in a dozen different directions, trying to think of a way to forgo the lecture that was surely headed his way.

"It's true, Micah." His *mammi* peered over her reading glasses at him. "There's no need to look hurt when your *daddi* is only stating the obvious. I spoke to your *dat* and *mamm* about this on several occasions."

"This?"

"She's referring to the way your *schweschdern* spoiled you—all of them did, really. It's not a surprise, you being the last child and only son."

Micah had seven older *schweschdern*, and it was true that they doted on him. He'd never washed a dish or helped prepare a meal. If he suddenly had to cook for himself, he'd probably perish from starvation. When he was young, he'd thought that was the life of every Amish boy, but as he grew older he'd learned his situation was a bit unique. The entire family had treated him as if he was a special gift left on the doorstep on Christmas morning.

Spoiled? *Ya.* He had been, but who in their right mind would turn that down? What was he supposed to do? Ask his siblings to be mean to him?

"You'll work with me in the fields every morning," his *daddi* continued. "There will be no more sleeping in."

Micah nearly choked on the sip of coffee he'd been in the process of swallowing. His *mammi* had called up the stairs at 5 a.m. sharp to wake him. That was sleeping in?

"After lunch you'll go to the bishop's and help in his farrier shop."

"The Beilers are *wunderbaar* people." His *mammi* might have winked at him, or she might have a twitch in her right eye. Micah couldn't tell. "This way you'll be learning two trades. Your *daddi* can teach you everything about farming—"

"Something your *dat* should have done already."

"And the bishop can teach you about horses."

As if he didn't know about horses. He was Amish, in spite of the way they were speaking to him. Micah felt the hairs on his neck stand on end, like a cat that had been brushed the wrong way. Why had he ever agreed to come to Indiana? What they were describing sounded worse than boot camp, which he only knew about from his friend Jackson, who had given him a ride from Maine.

Up before the birds.

Early-morning drills.

Work all day.

Collapse into bed at night.

Rinse and repeat.

His *daddi* gulped down the rest of his coffee, pushed his chair back and stood. The sleeve of his right arm had been sewn into a pocket, so that his stump rested inside it. He held his left hand in front of him—palm down—and made an invisible circle that included the three of them as well as the empty chairs, which he supposed his cousins had occupied before moving to Maine. In fact, it seemed the entire family was there, so what were his grandparents still doing in Goshen?

"We are your family—your *mammi* and me and all of your kinfolk here in Goshen. Your family in Maine loves you, as do we, but it's time for you to grow up, Micah. It's time to become a man."

And with that pronouncement, he turned and strode from the room.

Micah pulled in a deep breath, pushed himself away from the table and started across the room after him, but *Mammi* called him back.

"Best go upstairs and change first. I put proper clothing in your dresser and on the hooks. Your *daddi*—well, he won't abide the blue jeans and T-shirts."

The day seemed intent on continuing its slide from bad to worse.

"Anything else I should know? Any other changes I need to make?" He tried to sound lighthearted, but the words came out sarcastic and gruff. Too late to bite them back, and his *mammi* didn't seem to even notice.

"When you're done with the day's work, I'll cut your hair."

"What's wrong with my hair?"

"And he knows about the phone. As long as it isn't in the house—as long as he doesn't see it—he'll tolerate it. Just don't push him."

"I shouldn't push him?"

"He's old-fashioned, I know."

"You think?"

"But he's also a fair man." She stood and walked over to where he waited. His *mammi* barely reached his shoulders, but she was a formidable woman, and for some reason he couldn't identify, Micah wanted to make her proud. Reaching out, *Mammi* put a hand on his shoulder and waited until he met her gaze. "He's a *gut* man, and he cares about you. I suspect the changes will be difficult at first, but in the end, you'll thank him."

Micah seriously doubted that.

A quick glance at the clock told him it wasn't 6:30 a.m. yet.

The day was shaping up to be a long one.

He cheered himself with the thought that he only had 179 to go.

By the time they stopped for lunch, Micah was yawning and eyeing the hammock strung up in the backyard.

"Thomas expects you at one o'clock sharp, so you

best hurry." His *daddi* nodded toward the sandwich on Micah's plate. "You can eat that on your walk over."

Micah started to protest but then realized he'd probably prefer eating alone. At least he wouldn't have to listen to his *daddi*'s plans for their work the next day. He was too tired to even consider more fieldwork, and the day wasn't half-over.

Why had he never listened to the stories of how severe his *daddi* was?

If he had, he wouldn't have agreed to this exile.

He tried to hold on to his bad mood, but the weather was fabulous, and he had over a dozen comments on his social media pages. He'd fetched the phone from the barn as soon as he'd left the kitchen. He paused at the fence line long enough to answer the comments and snap another picture to post.

It would probably be a bad idea to take the phone over to the bishop's. Thomas Beiler was no doubt even more strict than Micah's *daddi*.

He glanced around for a place to hide it, but all he could see was fence line and fields, so he shoved it into his back pocket. Fortunately, on his way to the bishop's shop, he spied Susannah coming out of a small building set next to the house.

He called out to her and then jogged to where she was waiting.

"Do me a favor?"

"Like what?"

She was holding a basketful of fabric scraps. He pulled the phone from his pocket, picked up the stack of fabric and dropped the phone, then covered it back up. "Keep that for me until I'm done working."

"Why would I do that?"

"So I won't get in trouble on my first day in your *dat*'s shop."

"If you knew you would get in trouble, why did you—"

"Thanks, Susannah. You're a peach."

Instead of smiling, she glared at him, which caused him to laugh.

"I don't see what's so funny."

"You are. You just don't know it." He turned and walked backward so that he could point at her. "You're going to be my new best friend."

"Oh, I doubt that."

"You'll see."

"Uh-huh."

"Just don't use up all my battery playing *Candy Crush*."

"What is…"

But he never heard the rest because he realized it was five minutes past one and he was late. No doubt the bishop would relay that to his *daddi* and he'd be given extra chores, or perhaps they'd deliver yet another lecture. He absolutely hated lectures. It was difficult to sit there and act respectful and pretend to listen. He just did not understand old people. Best to avoid such a confrontation, so he broke into a run.

He was surprised when Thomas greeted him with a smile and no rebuke. "I was happy to hear you'd be here for a few months. I can use the help."

"Don't know as I'll be that much help."

"Does your mind work?"

"Excuse me?"

Thomas tapped the side of his head. He was tall for an Amish man, probably close to six feet. His beard was peppered with gray, and crow's-feet stretched out from his eyes. He struck Micah as a man who smiled easily.

"Does your mind work? How did you do in school?"

"Oh, I did fine."

"Then the work won't be too hard for you to learn. It's difficult physically… I'll give you that. But anyone who is willing to learn the trade will always have a job."

"*Ya*, always plenty of horses when Amish are around," Micah joked.

"Exactly. Now, let's get to work on Widower King's buggy horse."

Micah had never considered that he'd be straddling the leg of a thousand-pound beast. He'd lived around horses all of his life, but feeding a horse or harnessing it to a buggy was one thing. Getting that horse to raise its foot so you could trim away its hoof was another.

"A horse's hooves are like our fingernails. They must be trimmed and exfoliated." Thomas proceeded to show him how to cut off the excess growth, then clean and check the hoof for overall health. "It's important that the horse trusts you. If you appear confident and act like you know what you're doing, the horse will relax."

"But I don't know what I'm doing."

"You will. Soon enough you will. See this triangle-shaped thing at the bottom of the hoof?"

"Sure."

"That's the frog. It acts as a shock absorber of sorts. We need to clean it up. Don't want any ragged ends."

"Why?"

"*Gut* question. We clean it so the dirt and muck is able to get out of the foot easier. Next we trim the hoof wall. Hand me the curved blade there on the shelf."

Micah quickly did as asked. When Thomas was finished, he used a hoof nipper to trim the outside of the hoof wall, and then a rasp to even out everything.

"I never realized there was so much detail to shoeing a horse."

"Few people do—they count on their farrier. Think of it as job security." Thomas looked up and smiled. "Now let's see what sized shoes we need."

Susannah was tempted to find an excuse to visit her *dat*'s shop. How was Micah doing? And did he know anything about trimming hooves or shoeing horses? She knew firsthand that what her *dat* did was hard work. She'd sat in his workshop often enough and even helped him occasionally. She loved being around the animals whether they were buggy horses or workhorses.

It took her an hour to separate her fabric scraps by size and color. It was amazing what could be salvaged from one project to use in another. The process soothed her until she picked up the last piece of fabric and spied Micah's phone in the basket. Why did he have such a thing? How much did he pay for it? And who did he stay in touch with?

Other Amish rebels?

Someone in his family who had left the faith?

Or maybe an *Englisch* girlfriend?

She dropped the phone into her apron pocket. It didn't matter to her what Micah did with his phone, and she would set him straight that it wasn't her place to keep him out of trouble. She didn't think he was going to fit into their community very well. She didn't think he even wanted to.

There's a real possibility that what Micah needs most is not a girlfriend but simply a friend...

Remembering her *mamm*'s words caused her to feel a twinge of guilt. Perhaps he had a good reason for having the phone, though she couldn't imagine what that might be.

She didn't have to wait long to find out.

She was pulling laundry off the line while Shiloh and Sharon played on the trampoline when Micah came walking around the corner of the house.

He headed straight to the water hose and preceded to roll up his sleeves and wash his hands and arms. He even swiped some of the water on his neck, wetting the hair that curled there, and then he doused his face.

"We have indoor bathrooms."

"I like washing up with a water hose."

Susannah handed him a clean hand towel.

"Danki."

"Gem gschehne."

He rubbed his face dry, then his arms, and finally remembered that water was dripping down his neck. When he was finished, he held up the towel and asked, "Where should I—"

"I'll take it."

"Do you need help with the laundry?"

She inclined her head toward the empty clothesline.

"I could help fold."

"Do you know how to fold clothes?"

"How hard can it be?" He peeked into her basket. "Oh. Looks like you've already folded everything."

"It's easier to do while you pull the items off the line."

"I knew that."

"Sure you did." She moved closer to the trampoline so she could keep an eye on the girls.

Micah followed and plopped down on the grass. For

reasons she couldn't quite fathom, she did the same. It wasn't that she was interested in Micah, but she was curious as to what made him tick. How did he become so unorthodox? And why? What was the point of rebelling against their conventions?

"Actually, I know nothing about housework." He picked up their conversation as if there hadn't been a long, awkward silence. "I'm the baby of the family."

"Is that so?"

"Seven older *schweschdern*."

"What was that like?"

"I loved it, but apparently…according to my *daddi*, I was spoiled and it's time for me to grow up and become a man."

"Ouch."

"Yeah. Hence my exile here in Goshen for six months."

"When you say it that way, it sounds like a long time."

"It is a long time—a lifetime practically." Micah leaned forward and lowered his voice. "Not sure I'm going to make it if every day is like today."

"Why's that?"

"It's all so…grim."

The sun was setting in a beautiful splash of color, the horses were pastured in the field, Sharon and Shiloh played happily a few feet from her, and dinner was nearly done. "I don't understand."

"What?"

"Grim. How can you call this…" She took an exaggerated gaze around them. "How can you call it grim?"

"The work is endless."

"You didn't enjoy helping *Dat*?"

"Actually, that part was rather interesting."

"But…"

"But I'd already spent five hours in the field. I've done nothing but work all day. And tomorrow will be the same. It's just so…boring."

She fought the urge to defend their lifestyle, even their farm. So what if he didn't like it? Why should she care what Micah Fisher did and didn't like?

"If excitement is what you want, then *ya*, I agree that Goshen isn't the place for you."

"I knew you'd understand."

"And the work is endless because it's a farm. That's pretty much the definition of farmwork."

"I do not see the point."

Susannah didn't know what to say to that, so she asked, "How did it go working with *the horses*?"

"Better than I thought it would be. I only got kicked once."

"Once usually does the trick."

"You've helped your *dat* shoe horses?"

"Of course."

"Not exactly girl's work."

"So now you're a traditionalist?" She reached into her apron pocket, retrieved his phone and dropped it into his hand. "Except for that…"

"Have you ever owned a phone?"

"Nein."

"Did you play around on mine?"

"Of course not."

"It's not going to burn your fingers, you know."

"And yet it's forbidden."

"It's discouraged. There's a difference." He winked at her.

She refused to let his charm muddle her thoughts. "Does that usually work?"

"What?"

"Winking at girls."

"Not sure I wanted it to work. I was just being… friendly."

"Ah."

He stuffed the phone in his pocket and said, "*Ah*, what?"

"That's what people who flirt say…that they were just being friendly."

"So you think I was flirting with you?"

Susannah almost laughed, but she didn't want to encourage his silliness. The twins continued to jump on the trampoline, giggling and calling out to one another.

"Watch me, Susannah. I can flip." Sharon jumped and then fell onto her back. "Did I do it?"

"You didn't do it," Shiloh said.

"I did, too. Tell her, Susannah. Tell her I did."

"Almost. Keep practicing."

Micah flopped onto his back, staring up at the sky. "Your *dat* isn't what I expected."

"How so?"

"Well, he's a bishop."

"*Ya.*"

"I thought he'd be more conservative."

"Don't tell me he was watching TV again while shoeing the horses."

Micah propped himself up on his elbows, then smiled at the twins, who were trying to get his attention. "I mean he seems rather open-minded. He asked all about our community in Maine, which many of the old folks don't even want to know about. They think it's much too progressive."

"Is it?"

"I don't think so. Plus, look at this place." He waved at the backyard. "Trampoline for the kids."

"They need somewhere to play."

"A new little modular house."

"That's my sewing shop, where I quilt."

"I wondered what all those pieces of material were for."

"They're scraps and they're for sewing."

"Do you have an electric sewing machine in there?"

"I do not." Her cheeks warmed, not because he was teasing her but because of the way he was looking at her. She stood and picked up her laundry basket. "Dinner will be ready in a few minutes. I assume you're staying."

"I wouldn't miss it."

Sharon jumped closer to the edge of the trampoline and held onto the netting, which prevented her from falling out. "Come and jump with us, Susannah."

"Yeah, come and jump." Shiloh was actually sitting on the trampoline, not jumping. She was careful even there, as if the thing might throw her onto the ground.

"It's time to help with dinner. Come on inside."

"Just five more minutes…please."

It always made her smile how their voices could become one when they wanted something. Usually Sharon and Shiloh seemed like complete opposites, but when they joined together, they reminded her of two halves of the same whole.

"I have to go in, and you know *Mamm* doesn't like you out here alone."

"I'll stay with them," Micah said. "Unless you need me to help cook."

"Have you ever cooked before?"

"Nein."

"Then no—we don't need your help."

"I'll just stay here, then. I promise to keep an eye on them."

Actually, he did better than that. By the time she'd climbed the porch steps and looked back, Micah had removed his shoes and was pulling himself up onto the trampoline.

Not that he could ingratiate himself to her by playing with the girls. His comments had bordered on rude—first calling them progressive and then boring. Or, had it been the other way around? Regardless, he obviously didn't like it here and she didn't think he'd last even a week.

Which was absolutely fine with her.

The longer he stayed, the higher the risk he would be a bad influence on someone in their community. The last thing her friends needed was an Amish bad boy complete with long hair, *Englisch* phone, ball cap and blue jeans. Though he had been wearing more traditional clothes today. Where had those come from? Were they stuffed in his backpack?

Not her business.

She guessed he'd probably grow up eventually, but she didn't think it would be today or tomorrow or any-time in the near future.

That boy was trouble with a crooked smile.

The sooner Micah Fisher was out of their lives, the better. If he needed a friend, he could find one back home in Maine.

Chapter Three

By the time Sunday rolled around, Susannah's feelings regarding Micah had grown even more complicated. He'd shown up the second day with a fresh haircut but the same born-to-be-wild attitude. Her *dat* was happy with his work, but Susannah was growing increasingly uneasy around him. Micah reminded her of a wild horse temporarily corralled. It was only a matter of time before he broke out and then his grandparents would be heartbroken and her *dat* would be in need of another helper.

She spent much of the service praying that God would forgive her uncharitable feelings and clear the confusion in her mind. Since her *dat* was the bishop, she was aware that she was scrutinized more closely than others.

So even as her mind wandered toward Micah, she kept her attention on the person preaching.

When it was time to pray, she closed her eyes and petitioned her heavenly Father for clarity.

When it was time to sing, she stood and raised her voice with the others around her.

And as soon as the service ended, she hurried toward the serving area, not pausing to give their new neighbor a second glance. She worked at filling cups with water and lemonade. When she saw Micah walking toward her, she quickly changed tables to help with salads. It wasn't that she was avoiding him, but he would simply want to tell her more about Maine, a subject she'd heard quite enough about. When she finally had a few free moments, she snagged Deborah.

"Care to walk out into the pasture?"

"I can think of nothing I'd rather do." Deborah jumped up from her seat and grabbed her sweater from the big bag she carried around. Deborah was the only Amish person Susannah knew who carried what amounted to a baby bag though she had no baby. It was sometimes quite amazing what Deborah could pull out of that bag.

"Tell me about Micah," Deborah said as soon as they were out of earshot of the others.

"What's to tell?"

"Does he seem to be behaving himself?"

"*Dat* hasn't complained."

"I'm not surprised. Your father is the bishop. Of course Micah would be on his best behavior around him."

"*Ya*, I suppose."

"Betty heard that Micah had an alcohol problem when he was living in Maine. That's why his parents sent him here."

"Alcohol?"

"Or maybe it was drugs… She wasn't really sure."

Susannah sighed and pressed her lips together.

"You might as well say it," Deborah teased.

"Then I would be as bad as Betty."

"Oh. So you don't want to be a gossip, which you would be if you pointed out that Betty is a gossip."

That was such a convoluted statement that it made Susannah laugh, which helped her relax a little. "I guess I was thinking that Betty has been somewhat bitter since Joshua left the faith."

"And left her for an *Englisch* girl. I saw them in South Bend the other day."

"At the college?"

"*Ya.* They looked…um…close. Arms wrapped around each other. Kissing in public." Deborah made a wide-eyed, somewhat disgusted expression.

"Your *dat* is still consulting at the college?"

"He is. Their agriculture students want to know all about our Plain and simple ways."

Which caused them both to laugh.

"Perhaps they should come help in the fields—then they'd really understand."

"They're actually going to do that sometime in the next few weeks."

"Seriously?"

"Uh-huh."

"You're going to have *Englischers* traipsing around in your fields?"

"We are."

"Maybe we should send Micah over. He seems to speak their language."

They'd made it to the corner of the property where Mose King had made a bench out of a felled tree. After checking that there were no critters hiding beneath it, they both sat down and studied the scene in front of them.

Most of the women and a good number of the men were spread out in chairs under the trees.

Boys of all ages were playing baseball, with a few of

the men standing on the edge of the ball field, providing sideline advice.

The younger children were in a play area that Mose had made for his own children. It looked like a school playground. There was a seesaw, a swing set and even a sandbox that he kept covered with a tarp when it wasn't being used.

Susannah thought that playground was a sign of something—thoughtfulness, adoration, maybe devotion. "*Mamm* thinks Mose would make a *gut* husband."

"I'm sure he would...for someone his own age."

"*Ya*, my sentiments exactly."

"That's another thing I heard about Micah. He was apparently dating an older woman—who he dumped, and according to the grapevine, that wasn't the first relationship that he broke off for no reason."

"There's always a reason."

"I suppose."

"It's kind of sad that we're so interested in everything he did wrong there."

"Are you defending him?"

"Not at all. It's only that... Well, *Mamm* reminded me that everyone deserves a fresh start. Don't they?"

Deborah pulled her skirt up an inch or so and proceeded to pull stickers from her socks. "I guess. The only thing is that I'd rather these people who need a fresh start get it somewhere else."

Which pretty accurately mirrored Susannah's thoughts, though somehow, spoken out loud, they sounded rather judgmental and unfair.

"What do you mean?"

"I guess I was thinking that what Micah Fisher does in

Maine is his own business, but what he does here... Well, here he stands to hurt other people with his actions."

"Meaning what?"

Deborah shrugged and pretended to look for something in her purse. Susannah put her hand on top of the bag and left it there until her friend looked up.

"What aren't you telling me?"

"Apparently Micah sneaked out of his house on Friday night and met up with Caroline Byers."

"I have trouble believing that's true. He's been here less than a week. How could he—"

"I heard it from Caroline herself. She said it was harmless. Said they just happened to be downtown at the same time to hear a local band, but Betty heard them talk about meeting up again on Thursday."

Susannah had at least a dozen questions, but none of them really mattered. Most of them were none of her business. She settled for asking, "Her parents let her do that?"

"*Nein*. She sneaked out. Are you even paying attention?"

"I am now." Susannah jumped up, crossed her arms and paced back and forth in front of Deborah. "Caroline is young and impressionable. I can see how she'd fall for someone like Micah in a second, but I'm not sure that's a *gut* idea."

"Finally."

"Finally what?"

"Finally you're paying attention and concerned. I mean, the guy practically lives at your house. Maybe you could say something to him."

"I'm not sure that I could, or even that I *should*."

Deborah began to fiddle with her *kapp* strings, some-thing she only did when she was holding back.

"What else?"

"Well…one of the boys claimed they saw him smok-ing."

"He doesn't smell like smoke, and I should know… He's eaten with us three times now."

"There was also talk of his carrying a flask in the back pocket of those blue jeans and…you know…taking a sip now and again."

Susannah flopped back down beside Deborah. "I don't know if I'm more aggravated about the gossip—"

"Unless it's true."

"—or Micah's behavior."

That sat between them a few minutes until Susannah realized they needed to start back to help put out a snack for the children. It was nearly three in the afternoon and some of them would be going down for a nap soon.

They were halfway toward the main group when Deb-orah asked, "Are you going to talk to your *dat*?"

"*Nein*. He wouldn't want to hear about it unless it was something I saw myself. He has no patience for gossip." She turned abruptly so that Deborah nearly bumped into her. "If anyone else talks to you about Micah, about his behavior, you tell them to come to my *dat* directly. *Dat* will speak to him, but only if the report is a firsthand account."

"Okay. I should have done that to begin with. I guess I was a bit stunned by it all."

"Understandable, but now that we know about his reputation we need to take steps to protect our *freinden*."

"What kind of steps?"

"Well, I can keep a closer eye on him when he's at

our farm. I can certainly watch for the smoking and drinking."

"I doubt that he's likely to do either of those things around your *dat*."

"But there would be signs, and I just don't..." She looked toward the picnic tables, where she should be helping. Instead, she tugged on Deborah's arm and pulled her in the opposite direction. "It's just that I don't want him to be unfairly judged. He seems like a *gut* guy, just a bit lost."

"Reminds me of my *bruder* when he was on his *rumspringa*."

"Exactly."

"Only Elias was seventeen at the time."

"And Micah is twenty-five."

A shout rose up from the baseball field, where none other than Micah had apparently hit a home run and was jogging around the bases to the cheers of all watching.

Susannah pinched the bridge of her nose and squeezed her eyes shut. After taking a deep breath and letting it slowly out, she tried to shake off the feeling of trepidation. It was a beautiful Sunday afternoon, and so far at least, Micah had done nothing against their *Ordnung*— at least nothing she'd witnessed.

"We'll give him a fair chance but keep our eyes on him."

"Sounds reasonable." Deborah nodded so hard that her *kapp* strings bounced.

"And above all else, we'll make sure that he doesn't set his ball cap at any of the girls in our group."

"Like Betty."

"Or Caroline or any of the other girls we've grown

up with. The ones who aren't married... Well, some of them are too quick to fall in with a guy."

"Their biological clocks are going ticktock."

"Exactly."

Deborah tucked her arm through Susannah's. "The good part is that he's not planning on staying, from what I've heard."

"He said as much to me, as well. Hopefully he can serve his time at his *daddi*'s and then go home to break hearts."

"*Gut* idea. We don't need any of that sort of drama around here."

Which echoed what Susannah had been thinking. Personally, she'd experienced enough tragedy in the last few years with her cancer diagnosis, treatment and the breakup with Samuel. She knew firsthand what it was like to have your dreams ripped away, to have your heart shredded to the point that it felt raw. If she had anything to do with it, that would not be happening to her friends. Even if it meant she had to take matters into her own hands.

The following Thursday, Micah had finished shoeing a dappled gray mare under the watchful gaze of Thomas. Then the bishop had been called off to visit with one of the old-timers who had taken a turn for the worse, and before Micah knew it, he was being babysat by Susannah.

"I can take the man's money and put it in the box."

"What man?"

"The man who owns the mare."

"Yes, but you don't even know the man's name. Mr. Hochstetler has been bringing his horses here since I was a *kind. Dat* likes for our customers to have personal service."

"They're Amish. Where else are they going to go to have their horses cared for?"

"Not the point, according to *Dat*. The point is that we treat every customer as if we value their business—which we do."

"Fine. I didn't remember the man's name, but you could tell me that and leave."

"Do you know the mare's name?"

"*Nein* and what difference does that make? Are you going to tell me that the mare needs to feel valued, too?"

"Of course she needs to be valued. Have you ever owned a mare?"

"Never needed to. I had my parents' buggy horses to use in Maine, and I have my grandparents' here."

"But one day you'll be a man with your own family and your own horses." Susannah had been grooming the mare, which definitely did not fall under the services of shoeing a horse in Micah's opinion. She stopped what she was doing and pointed the brush at him. "When you have your own horses, you'll understand why it's important to appreciate them and treat them with respect."

Micah rolled his eyes and then started laughing. He couldn't help it.

"What?"

"Nothing."

"Just say it."

"You couldn't even see over that horse if you weren't standing on a crate, and yet you're lecturing me."

"What does being short have to do with anything?"

Micah raised his hands in surrender, but he continued to laugh. Most days Susannah aggravated him, especially when she reminded him of his nagging sisters. But then, other times, he caught a glint of mischievousness in her eyes, and he wondered what else was going on underneath her perfectly starched *kapp*.

"Say, I'm thinking about asking Caroline Byers to this weekend's spring festival in town. What do you think?"

"Terrible idea." Susannah resumed brushing the mare, but much more vigorously.

"Why's it terrible?"

Now her lips were forming a tight, straight line, as if they'd been glued together. He knew that expression well enough.

"Just say it. What's the problem?"

"She's too young for you, that's what!" Susannah brushed the mare so vigorously that it turned its large muzzle toward her. "Sorry, Smokey."

"Smokey?"

"That's her name. If you'd bothered to find out, you would know that."

"You seem awfully cranky all of a sudden."

"I'm not cranky!" She jumped off the crate, cleaned the horse brush with a metal tool and slammed it onto the tool shelf. Next she picked up the currying comb, which looked somewhat dangerous the way she was brandishing it in his direction. "Pick a girl your age, Micah."

"Wow. Okay. Well, I hadn't thought of it that way, but I guess I see your point. How about Betty Gleich?"

Susannah closed her eyes as if praying for patience and shook her head so hard he feared her *kapp* would pop off.

"What's wrong with Betty? I know for a fact she's over twenty-one."

"She's twenty-two, and she just went through a rather rough breakup."

"What does that have to do with me?"

"Did you not say only twenty minutes ago that you only had—and I quote—one hundred and seventy days left in this awful place?"

"Sounds like something I might have said."

"Obviously you hate it here."

"You don't understand. If you'd been to Maine, then you'd appreciate how much more beautiful it is than your much-loved Indiana. If you could experience the hunting, the fishing, the wildness of the place. It's just—"

"You'd be in your precious Maine right this minute if you hadn't been banished."

"Ouch."

"Again—your word, not mine."

"Fine." He named off four other perfectly eligible girls, all of whom Susannah disapproved of him dating for the most ridiculous reasons and sometimes for no reason she'd share at all.

His mounting frustration was threatening to get the better of him. He tried to mentally order himself to calm down, but the way Susannah was frowning at him was not helping matters. "What is your problem?"

"My problem?"

"You know, I don't need your permission to date someone, but now I'm curious. What's your beef?"

"Beef?"

"Apparently I'm not *gut* enough for any of the gals in your district."

"It's not a question of whether you're *gut* enough for them."

"Then what?"

"You're leaving, that's what. You're leaving, and they'll get attached to you, and then it will hurt them when you go."

"I'm not proposing to them, Susannah. I'm asking them out on a buggy ride."

"One thing leads to the other."

Micah threw up his hands and walked out of the farrier shop. The sky was dark and brooding, a perfect reflection of his mood. Well, Susannah Beiler was not the boss of him. He could ask out whomever he liked.

He stomped back in to tell her that and caught her with her cheek pressed against the mare, a look of utter desolation in her eyes. Now he felt like a heel, and he didn't even know what he'd done.

"Hey…it's not that bad."

She stood up straighter, gave the mare one last pat and returned the crate to its place along the wall.

"You can't expect a guy to hang around for six months and not go on a single date. Surely you can see that."

"Why?"

"Why? Because it's not natural."

"There's nothing wrong with being alone, Micah."

"Maybe not for you, but I haven't decided I want to be single the rest of my life—apparently you have."

"This discussion isn't about me."

Now her chin rose as if she needed to defend herself—oh, the many faces of Susannah Beiler. If she ever came down from her high horse, she might be an interesting person to get to know.

"Look, I'm sorry." He yanked off his hat and stared at it—a straw Amish hat. Why couldn't he wear his ball cap? Glancing up, he realized Susannah was waiting.

He forced himself to refocus on the problem at hand. "I didn't mean to offend you, but you're so…"

"What?"

"Serious. You're so serious, and life is just waiting for us to enjoy it." In three long strides, he was at her side. Grasping her by the shoulders, he marched her toward the open barn door. "See that? The clouds and the rain and the turbulence?"

"I see it."

"But behind all of that are more things that we can't begin to imagine—sunshine and new experiences and memories waiting to be made. Life is out there, Susannah. We're supposed to be living it."

"And you can't do that without dragging some poor girl along with you?"

"Why should I?"

Susannah rubbed at her forehead as if she'd quite suddenly been slapped with the worst headache imaginable. Finally, she pulled in a deep breath and turned to stare up into his face.

"Then take me."

"Huh?"

"If you must take someone on these jaunts around our little town, take me."

"But…you don't even like me."

"That's beside the point."

"No, I think that is the point."

"You're not looking for love, Micah. We both know that. You're looking for a buddy to pal around with, and there are plenty of men your age in our district."

"All paired up. I've already tried that route."

"Then take me, like I said."

"You're going to pal around with me? Miss Susannah

Beiler, who does everything by the book? That should be a load of fun."

"I do not do everything by the book."

"You cleaned the horse brush before putting it on the shelf. Who does that?"

"You're changing the subject. Is it a deal or not?"

"A deal?"

"I go with you to enjoy life, and you leave the girls in my district alone."

"Wow. There's a proposal that is hard to turn down."

"So it's a deal."

She held out her hand, which reminded him of meeting her out on the lane, offering his hand and her refusing it. He couldn't help laughing as he clasped her small hand in his large one.

"Fine. It's a deal, but you're going to regret it."

"I have no doubt that is true." And then she turned and strode toward the house.

"I thought you needed to be here when Mr. Hochstettler came by," he called out to her.

Rather than bothering to answer, she simply gave him a backward wave.

So, he was going to date the bishop's daughter.

Or rather, *not* date her.

It would be like having a chaperone along every time he went to town. He kicked the door of the barn, startling the mare.

"Easy, Smokey. It's just me, doing a stupid thing to top off another stupid thing."

One hundred and seventy days.

Somehow, that seemed like an even longer stretch of time than it had an hour ago.

Chapter Four

Susannah went with Micah to hear a music duo on Friday. She had to resist the urge to remind him that they were Amish and their *Ordnung* strongly discouraged listening to worldly music. But she didn't have to point that out. Micah taunted her with it as soon as they were in the buggy and driving away from her parents' farm.

"Guess your *mamm* and *dat* didn't want you to go tonight."

"Why would you say that?"

"First of all, because it's with me."

"For reasons I can't fathom, my parents have taken a real liking to you."

"Huh." He looked pleased for a brief moment, but then he slouched his shoulders and rammed his hat down on his head. "Wish I could say the same for my *daddi*."

"I'm sure your *daddi* likes you."

"*Nein*. He might love me. He's supposed to love me, but like me? I'm pretty sure that isn't the case."

"Why would you say that?"

"A guy can tell."

"Give me an example."

"Okay." He pulled the buggy out onto the main road, then glanced at her and smiled, as if he was sure he could prove his point—even though his point was that his own *daddi* didn't like him. "I asked him to go fishing, and he said no."

"Maybe he was tired."

"I asked him to play checkers, and he said no."

"Maybe he's not good at checkers and hates losing."

"I even asked him if he'd like to walk outside with me and see an owl's nest that I found."

"Maybe he doesn't like owls."

Micah laughed, stretched like a cat and looked immensely proud of himself. "Enough about my problems, but admit that your parents did not like the idea of your going to an *Englisch* concert."

Susannah shrugged and refused to make eye contact.

"Oh, my gosh. You never had a *rumspringa*!"

She shook her head and closed her eyes. He really was incorrigible. She wasn't about to explain that she'd been going through her cancer diagnosis and treatment when her friends were enjoying their running-around time.

"I hit the nail on the head. I knew they didn't approve of your going to hear Jason Wright and the Red River Posse band."

"What does that even mean? Red River Posse?"

"Well, a posse is a group of individuals who are sort of deputized. You know, they help out the sheriff."

"And Red River?"

"In Texas."

"And Jason Wright?"

"I think it's a play on the word *right*, like being right, not wrong."

"Ridiculous."

"Uh-huh." Now he did looked pleased. "Just as I thought. You're going to hate it."

"I might not hate it. I happen to like music."

"You do?"

"Sure. I've been known to hum a melody as I sew."

"What kind of melody?"

"Uh...the only kind I know. Songs from church." She rushed on when he gave her an I-told-you-so look. "That's not the point. Did you specifically pick this to do tonight because you thought I'd hate it? Are you trying to—" she waved a hand at the passing roadside "—ditch me?"

"Oh, no. You're not getting out of this that easily by saying that I'm trying to ditch you. Uh-uh. I'm not ditching anyone. I'm glad that the bishop's daughter is having a night out on the town. Besides, you're my only option if I'm not allowed to date anyone else."

"I'm not the boss of you, Micah."

"Exactly. But you know how to put the pressure on, just like a woman."

"Oh, good grief."

"So if I'm being pressured not to date other girls in your community, then you have to stick to our deal."

"Fine by me."

They rode in silence for a minute, but then Micah returned to his original question. "So, were your parents upset...about where we were going?"

"*Nein.* I'm a grown woman. I can go wherever I want."

"But you've already joined the church."

"Which doesn't mean I can't enjoy an evening in the park."

"Uh-huh."

"If a band happens to be playing, there's no rule that says I have to cover my ears."

"I see."

"It's not like I have a radio hidden away in my sewing room."

"Already I'm corrupting you."

She slapped his arm, but in truth it was a relief to get away from the farm for an evening. It had been a long time since she'd done something that didn't involve her family or her girlfriends or her sewing. She loved all those things, but it felt good to do something different. Maybe Micah was a bad influence or maybe he could be for some people, but she would be more careful than that. She had decided not to worry about anything this evening.

She actually had fun at the park. There were booths set up where people were selling homemade items like jewelry and T-shirts and even ball caps. Micah put one over her *kapp* that was pink and had the word *Princess* spelled out in glitter. Susannah told the woman it was beautiful and carefully placed it back on the table.

The local pizzeria had a booth where they were selling giant slices, but Micah insisted on buying a large pizza. Susannah couldn't remember the last time she'd eaten two slices of pizza, but when Micah dared her to eat another piece she actually found she was still hungry. Maybe it was from all the walking around they'd done.

And the music wasn't so bad. They saw a few other Amish families enjoying the fine May evening, though none were actually sitting up front listening to the band like they were. She waved each time she saw someone from their district.

"What's wrong?" Micah nudged his shoulder against

hers. "I rather liked that song. It was all about bull riding, which I saw once in Maine. Maybe you'd prefer love songs."

"Oh, it's not that. I waved at the Kings."

"Mose King? Isn't he the one you told me was a widower? The guy your *mamm* wants you to marry? Point him out to me. I want to see if he has hair sprouting out of his ears and uses a cane."

She slapped his arm. "Not Mose, his brother and sister-in-law—Frank and Ida. I waved when they looked toward us, but they turned away as if they didn't see me."

"They probably didn't see you." Micah nodded his head to the left and right. "Lots of people here."

"I guess you're right."

He pulled back and widened his eyes in mock surprise. "Excuse me? Could you say that again?"

Which made her laugh, and then she stopped worrying about the Kings.

Susannah helped her mother clean their house the next day. Since it wasn't a church weekend, they were having dinner for their closest neighbors—which would include Micah and his grandparents.

"I'm interested to see how they react around him," she confessed to her mother as she dumped the pail of dirty water on the flower beds.

"What do you mean?"

"Well, according to Micah, his *mammi* is strict but kind."

"Abigail is a *gut* woman."

"But his *daddi* is beyond strict. Micah says he doesn't think his *daddi* cares for him very much."

"Why would he say such a thing?"

Susannah shrugged, then plopped down beside her mother in the porch swing. The twins were playing with a set of jacks on the far side of the porch. The sight of their heads nearly touching as they leaned over the jacks and ball made Susannah extremely happy. Was it just two years ago that she was worried she wouldn't see them grow up to be young girls? Yet, here they were. She was thankful for that, for every day she had with her family.

"Where'd you go?" her *mamm* asked softly.

"Just thinking about how grateful I am to still be alive."

"I thank the Lord for that very thing every day when I rise and every evening when I go to sleep. It's a frightening experience to almost lose a child."

Susannah cornered herself in the swing so she could study her mother. "I guess it's easy for me to forget how hard that time was on you."

"That's the thing… When tragedy is in our past we do forget about it, but it changes us, Susannah. Just like you are a more serious young woman—a more grateful and mature one—because of your illness. I'm changed, too, as is your *dat*. We realize more than we ever did before how precious each day is."

They pushed the swing for a while as the girls' laughter spilled toward them. Susannah's mind drifted back toward Micah and his grandfather. As if sensing the turn in her thoughts, her *mamm* stood up and brushed dirt off her apron. "John Fisher loves Micah. I have no doubt about that. I didn't know him before the accident…"

"The one where he lost his arm?"

"*Ya.* I didn't know him then, but I imagine it changed him just as your experience with cancer changed you. We can never know how a person's path through this life twists and turns. We only know where they are right now. But John? Well, it's been hard for him."

"Because of his disability."

"That and probably how strangers look at him—no one wants to be pitied."

"I hated when people looked at me that way—when I was going through the worst of the chemo."

"John has endured those looks all of his life. People mean well, but sometimes they allow your disability to define you, and none of us want that." She reached for Susannah's hand and pulled her off the swing. As they walked inside to prepare lunch, she added a final comment on the subject. "John does love Micah. Abigail has shared with me that they are both worried about the boy, and John intends to do his best by him. Sometimes that's not an easy thing."

That evening Micah took her moonlight fishing. As they walked across the back fields to the pond, Susannah felt as light as one of the swallows darting through the last of the sunset. She realized in that moment that she felt happy, really happy for the first time in a long time. Glancing at Micah, she wondered if that had anything to do with him.

But that thought was ridiculous.

It wasn't Micah that was changing the way she looked at things.

But it could be that doing things she wasn't used to—going to the park and listening to bands and fishing in the moonlight—was pulling her out of a lingering depression that had started when she'd first been diagnosed.

"Tell me you're not thinking of changing your mind."

Micah shifted the backpack across his shoulders. "I even brought *Mammi*'s cookies and coffee."

"I'm not going to change my mind, but I don't believe we'll catch anything. You can't fish by moonlight."

"Can, too."

"How do you know if you've caught anything?"

Micah reached into his pocket and pulled something out. As he shook his closed fist, she heard a jingle sound.

"Bells?"

"Yup. Small ones." He was carrying two fishing poles, and he waved them in front of him. "Plus, I rigged these up with fluorescent line."

"Now, that was a waste of money."

"You won't think so when we catch a lot of fish."

They didn't catch a lot of fish, but somehow that didn't matter too much to Susannah. Sitting on the dock in the moonlight, she thought that she hadn't ever seen a more beautiful evening. The moonlight resembled the soft glow from a lantern. If she focused, she could just make out the fishing line stretched out from Micah's poles. He'd attached the bells on the end, and each time they rang she laughed.

"You're scaring off the fish."

"I'm sorry, but I've never fished with a bell before."

"Have you ever fished before?"

"Some." She almost said "before my cancer," but then she realized she hadn't told him about that part of her life. Did he know? Had someone else told him? Maybe not. Maybe that was why she liked being around him. Micah didn't treat her as if she might break.

A few minutes earlier she'd thought he was going to make good on his threat to push her into the water. He'd only stopped when she'd grabbed one of the poles and said she'd take it with her. She enjoyed people treating her like a normal person. Maybe that was what she'd been missing.

"Oatmeal cookie for your thoughts?" He held up a cookie, and when she reached for it, he moved it out of her reach. "Uh-uh, you have to tell me what you were thinking about first."

"Right. Okay. Well, I was thinking about something my *mamm* said, that hard times change a person."

"Ya?" He handed her the cookie and then scooted the thermos of decaf coffee closer to her. "What kind of hard times?"

"I guess it could be anything, but the point is that you're not the same afterward. Maybe you start out carefree and end up serious. Or maybe you start out sure of everything, every turn your life is going to take. Like you have it all planned out. You know?"

"I've never planned much," Micah admitted.

"Say you did, and then something happened to change everything."

"Everything?"

"Ya."

"Huh. I guess that would make me more cautious." He reeled in a little of the fishing line, then asked, "Is that what happened to you? Is that why you're such a rule follower?"

"I'm not a very good rule follower. I went to a concert with you last night."

"And it didn't corrupt you a bit."

"True, but I need to be careful, or I might start singing about pickup trucks and mud on my boots."

She picked up one of her flip-flop sandals, waved

it at him and then sat it back down. "Imagine that—an Amish woman in cowgirl boots."

Micah picked up the other shoe and studied it. "This looks nothing like a boot. Maybe if I threw it into the water, it would change and become a boot."

"Give me that shoe back."

But Micah had already jumped up and was holding the flip-flop over his head. "This? You want this?"

"Micah, don't you dare…"

"Sounds like you're issuing an ultimatum."

"I need that shoe to walk back to the house. You don't want me walking barefoot through the fields."

"It's good for a person to walk barefoot. Helps you to feel connected to *Gotte*'s green earth."

Susannah was standing on her tiptoes, trying to wrestle the shoe from his hands, and Micah was moving backward to avoid her, a big dopey grin on his face. Then he took one too many steps backward at the exact moment that she rested a hand on his chest so she could keep her balance and reach up higher with the other hand. His eyes found hers just before they splashed into the water.

She came up sputtering, shocked that she was now thoroughly wet. Then she heard something that was becoming quite familiar to her—Micah's laughter.

He pointed at her head. "You have moss on top of your *kapp*."

"Oh, so you think that's funny. Is that why you're laughing?" She reached down into the water, grabbed a fistful of the slimy green stuff, then lurched toward him and tossed it on top of his head. After that, it was rather a free-for-all of water splashing and moss throwing.

Micah was the one who noticed that her flip-flop had drifted toward the middle of the pond. He swam out to it with sure, easy strokes. She waited near the dock in the moonlight, standing in water up to her waist and wondered where he'd learned to swim like that. His shadow in the moonlight reminded her of a large fish cutting through the water.

It occurred to her that Micah was a nice guy and a good-hearted man. He was certainly not difficult to look at. That thought caused her cheeks to burn with embarrassment, and she was grateful for the darkness. He wasn't interested in her, and she certainly wasn't interested in him—not that way. They were just hanging out together, helping him through a tough time until he was able to return home. She'd do well to keep that thought front and center.

When he returned and presented her with the shoe, she grabbed it from him with what she hoped was a curt "I'm going to get even for this."

Walking out of the water, she paused at the edge to put her shoes on her feet and squeeze water from her dress. She didn't realize he was behind her until he spoke— his mouth close to her ear and his words a mere whisper that sent goose bumps down her arms. "You look awfully pretty in the moonlight, Susannah Beiler."

Which set off every emotional alarm she possessed.

Was he flirting with her?

Did he think she had been flirting with him?

What was she doing standing in the moonlight with Micah Fisher? She was supposed to be keeping an eye on him—keeping him out of trouble.

Before she could work any of that out, Micah said, "Let me gather up our stuff. Then we can walk back by the road. It'll give our clothes time to dry off a bit."

The route would be longer, but Susannah found she didn't mind.

A small part of her wished the night could go on and on.

Micah whistled through his Sunday morning chores, maybe because he knew they were going over to the Beilers for lunch. There was something about Susannah that intrigued him. It wasn't that he was falling for her—she was much too serious to be his type—but she was easy to be around.

And she was a challenge.

He was honest enough to admit that he loved a good challenge.

The morning devotion time with his grandparents was a bit trying. His *daddi* had an obvious focus in mind. They began in the book of Psalms, reading how *Gotte* would establish the work of their hands—whatever that meant. Then moved to Proverbs, where they spent a good twenty minutes on a verse about sluggards and how such persons were doomed to an unsuccessful life. Finally, they ended up in Colossians, where Paul wrote that whatever they did they should do with all their heart.

Micah tried to stay focused.

He didn't fidget or peek at the clock in the kitchen even once.

But he did feel resentment building in his soul. Did he not work hard every single day? What did his grandfather want from him? And why had his parents banished him to Indiana when it was obvious that he belonged in Maine?

By the time they'd finished the final prayer, Micah was feeling agitated and needing to burn off some steam.

He felt like he could hit a baseball a hundred times and still have energy to spare.

"We'll be driving the buggy over to the Beilers' place." His *mammi* had followed him into the mudroom, where he'd grabbed his hat and jammed it on his head.

"*Danki, Mammi*, but I'll walk."

He didn't wait for an answer.

He didn't bother to explain.

He needed out of there and away from their disapproving stares.

Being outside in the sunshine helped. He wasn't normally a morose person. Sometimes, though, he felt backed into a corner. For the life of him, he could not understand what people wanted from him, what they expected. He chewed on those thoughts for the first half of his walk, but as soon as Susannah's little sewing shop came into view, his mood improved.

Last night had been fun.

He'd almost kissed her just to see what it would be like.

But the way her eyes had widened... Well, it had caused him to pat her awkwardly on the arm and walk away.

Had Susannah never been kissed?

Why wasn't she dating?

She was a smart girl with a pleasant personality. She apparently was a very good quilter, as there were often people stopping at her little shop to purchase quilts. She was patient with her sisters, and she was pretty to boot.

Why wasn't she married?

He forgot that question and his aggravation with his grandparents as soon as he started helping Susannah carry out food to the picnic tables. Her little sisters—

Sharon and Shiloh, who looked so much alike that he still couldn't tell them apart—had taken a liking to him. They followed him like baby ducks waddling after their mama.

In truth, they reminded him of his own *schweschdern* back in Maine—they were older, but he rather missed having them around. He could always make them laugh, and they thought he was ever so clever.

Shiloh and Sharon helped him and Susannah set up a volleyball net.

They insisted on showing him the new kittens in the barn and the baby goats in the pasture.

They sat beside him as everyone ate lunch.

"You need to finish eating, Sharon." Susannah nodded toward her sister's plate with a stern look.

Which, of course, made Micah laugh because Susannah looked so serious and Sharon looked so frustrated. And then he remembered that Sharon was the one always running ahead. She also had freckles sprinkled across her cheeks and the bridge of her nose.

"Why are you laughing at me, Micah? I don't want to eat. I want to play."

"*Ya*, but the playing is not going anywhere, and you need to eat to have lots of energy."

"*Mamm* always says I have plenty of energy."

"That's because you knock things over a lot," Shiloh commented as she was carefully attempting to cut a piece of ham with a knife and fork.

"Want some help with that?" he asked.

She nodded enthusiastically, but Susannah shook her head in disapproval. "How will she ever learn?"

"How will she learn what?"

"*If* you do it for her, how will she learn?"

"I'm watching him do it, Susannah."

"*Ya*, you're watching, but your hands are smaller. When your hands are bigger you'll be able to do it yourself."

Shiloh studied her palms, then held them up for all to see. "Still small."

He couldn't have said why he felt so comfortable around Susannah and her sisters, but the afternoon flew by. Micah's grandparents left early, *Mammi* claiming she had a terrible headache.

"Is she okay?" Susannah asked.

"She gets migraines sometimes. Says the only thing to do for them is lie down in a dark room."

"Should you have gone home with them?"

"They'd probably rather I didn't." He laughed at the look of dismay on Susannah's face. "What I mean is that it's quieter when I'm not there."

"How much noise do you make?"

"Not that much, but they're used to living alone."

"How did they end up here without any family?"

"Their oldest daughter—my *aenti* Grace—married and moved to Maine when the Unity community was first established in 2008."

"How did she happen to meet a fellow from Maine?"

"Her husband, Otis, had been looking for cheaper land, moving every few years, trying to find a less crowded area. Lots of eligible men in Maine and not a lot of women, since the communities are smaller. My other *aentis* had soon married and moved there, as well. Then my *dat* would visit, and the way he tells it, he loved being out in the wild. In fact, that's our family motto. It's sort of a joke. *Less people and more wild animals*."

Susannah rolled her eyes and shook her head at the same time. Ha! He was getting to her.

"My *dat* says he wouldn't want to live anywhere else, that he's glad I grew up there."

"But you weren't born there?"

"*Nein*. I was actually born in Wisconsin."

"Wisconsin?"

"Before he settled on Maine, my parents moved every few years. According to my *mamm*, they'd move to a place, get settled and then the community would double in size and my *dat* would start looking in the *Budget* for another place to move."

"So why haven't your *daddi* and *mammi* moved to be with the rest of the family?"

"That's a really good question, one that I've been asking myself, but I haven't figured out the answer. Maybe they were waiting to see if we'd all actually stay there."

"Sounds like your *dat* plans on staying."

"*Ya*, he does. The problem is that the other communities in Maine are quite strict. Fort Fairfield, which is the northernmost district, was originally a Swartzentruber district."

"I've heard of them. More conservative?"

"Much. They're not allowed to hire drivers unless it's for an emergency, no close relationships with non-Amish people and their clothes are even more Plain." He bumped his shoulder against hers as they walked toward the adjacent field. "That pretty peach color you're wearing wouldn't be allowed."

"I can't imagine you living in a community that strict."

"Well, where we live in Unity isn't that strict, but there's still the influence of the other groups."

"Maybe that's why you're such a renegade."

"I'm a renegade?" He stopped in his tracks, hands

on his hips. "You have offended me deeply, Susannah Beiler."

"Sure I did."

They walked to an old swing suspended from a tall maple tree. "Have a seat."

"What?"

"Sit down. I'll push you."

"You want me to get in the swing?"

"Sure and certain. It'll make you feel free. Make you feel as if you could touch the sky." He stepped closer. Already he was learning that she spooked easily. Susannah was accustomed to her personal space. Anytime he stepped within that space, she looked like a colt about to bolt. Rather than let him in her space, she plopped down into the swing and raised her feet.

"So push me already."

Soon they were both laughing, and Micah was wondering if he could talk her into fishing again. But they were interrupted by Sharon, who ran up and said, "*Dat* wants to see you both. In the house."

"Are we in trouble?" He was kidding, but the look on Sharon's face said that he might have nailed it with his question.

"Both of us?" Susannah asked.

"*Ya*, that's what he said. I have to go. We found a bird nest over by the barn, and I'm watching the babies try to fly." She fairly screamed the last part as she ran in the opposite direction.

"Does she ever slow down?"

"Only when she's sleeping."

Apparently their afternoon free time was over. Micah pulled Susannah to her feet, and they trudged toward the house, in step with one another.

"Any idea what this is about?" He tried not to sound worried. Why should he be worried? It wasn't as if he'd never been called in to see the bishop before. He should have expected this, though somehow he'd begun to hope that things could be different in Goshen.

"Nein."

"Your *dat* didn't say anything at breakfast?"

She shook her head, glancing at the adults gathered around the picnic table.

When they walked into the house and saw that Thomas was there with one of the other preachers—some guy by the name of Atlee—Micah sensed they were in trouble. He could understand why he might be. Not that he could think of anything in particular, but there was always something. It was actually rather a surprise that he'd made it nearly two weeks without being reprimanded by someone.

But Susannah? He couldn't imagine why she'd been called in.

"Have a seat." Thomas indicated the couch, so they sat side by side. Thomas sat in a rocker, and Atlee was in a rather large upholstered chair. He was a small older man, and the chair pretty much dwarfed him.

"I'll get right to the point," Thomas said. "I've had two different families come to me this morning with concerns about your behavior."

"Mine?" Susannah's voice screeched like a hoot owl.

It made Micah smile, which caused Atlee to frown.

Micah quickly schooled his expression in an attempt to appear more serious.

"Can't think of any reason there would have been concerns," Micah said. "I pretty much just worked all week."

"And I was working on that new quilt order I had."

"I'm sure you both did work very hard." Thomas's expression softened. "This was about the weekend, beginning with Friday night at the park."

Susannah crossed her arms and frowned. "I can't think of anything we did wrong at the park."

"Perhaps we shouldn't think of this as right or wrong, but rather something that someone saw and was concerned about. You two are old enough to realize that it matters how we're perceived by the community at large. We're to be examples of Christ, and we're to set ourselves apart from the world."

"Of course." Micah stared at the floor, because if he looked up, Thomas would see that he was about to lose his temper. He just had no patience for this sort of thing.

"You went to the park in town?" Thomas asked.

"*Ya.* I told you that, *Dat.* You said it would be fine."

"And you stayed to hear the concert?"

"In fact you moved and sat up front, if accounts are correct." Atlee studied them through large round glasses.

Micah blew out a noisy breath, then he sat up straighter. "We did, and I asked Susannah if it was all right before we did so."

"And I told him it was. *Dat*, there's nothing wrong with listening to music. We didn't get up and dance. We didn't waste money on a CD that we could bring home and play on a hidden music player we keep in the barn."

Thomas sighed heavily, then scooted to the edge of the rocker, his elbows braced on his knees.

"Why do we sing?"

Micah glanced up, wondering if this was a trick question. He was surprised to see a twinkle in Thomas's eyes when he'd expected to see condemnation.

"To express our moods," Micah said.

"Because it lifts our spirits," Susannah added.

"All right. Those are both *gut* reasons. But you've forgotten the Biblical reason—to give glory to *Gotte*. Singing, it's an act of worship, just like when we pray or observe communion or when we wash one another's feet."

Micah shifted uncomfortably in his seat. He wasn't sure where Thomas was going with this. This wasn't the standard lecture he'd received back home from his bishop or his *dat* or even from his *daddi*.

"We're even admonished to keep singing in the Bible. Paul told us to encourage one another with psalms and hymns and spiritual songs." Thomas paused, then added, "I suspect that isn't what you were listening to at the park."

"Nein," Susannah said softly.

"More like songs about pickup trucks and mud and boots."

"Ah." Thomas slapped his leg, as if they were finally getting to the crux of the matter. "We could relate to that if it was a buggy instead of a pickup truck."

When Micah dared to look at him again, he was grinning. "We want to be separate from the world, though I've been known to listen to a country tune myself once in a while. You both know Jethro. He gives rides to Amish folk, always has his radio turned to country music. I heard a lady named Alison Krauss sing 'Amazing Grace' once. It was beautiful indeed."

"So why are we in trouble?" Micah asked.

"I didn't say you were. I only said people were concerned."

"Then there's the matter of last night." Atlee cleared

his throat and pushed up his glasses. "Perhaps we should move on to that."

"All we did last night was fish, *Dat*. You knew we were going to do that. You even reminded me not to get my line caught up in the brush."

"This has more to do with you coming home in the dark at a very late hour, apparently in clothes that were soaking wet."

And there it was. The line they had crossed. Micah knew that he always managed to find it, but this time he'd dragged Susannah with him.

Thomas spent the next twenty minutes leading them through scripture that directed them to be separate, to be set apart, to be holy. By the time he finished, Micah was feeling appropriately chastised. He thought it might end there, but then Thomas stood and delivered his final decree. "Perhaps we should continue this conversation after you've had some time to think on it. I believe a weekly meeting might be appropriate—between the three of us. Do you agree, Susannah?"

"Sure."

"Micah?"

What could he do? Micah agreed. He couldn't leave Susannah to endure the punishment alone, though spending an hour each week being lectured didn't sound like his idea of fun. At least it would be with Thomas and not Atlee. If he'd been told he had to spend an hour with the frowning old guy, he might have been tempted to throw in the towel and walk back to Maine.

Chapter Five

The Goshen Amish community held a barn raising on Friday and Saturday of the following week. Of course, Micah had been to plenty of barn raisings and home raisings, too, for that matter. In Maine, their community was small, which meant that everyone pitched in when there was a need. But the fact that they were small also meant that raisings took a week to complete. Everyone showed up on the first day and then people worked on it as they were able throughout the week until it was completed. Apparently in Goshen they did things differently.

He dropped his grandparents off near the main house, then parked the buggy.

"Where did all these people come from?" he asked Elias Yoder, who was directing buggies.

"There are twenty thousand Amish in Elkhart and Lagrange counties."

"And they're all here today?"

Elias laughed as he chalked a number on Micah's grandfather's buggy—#321. *Wow.* There were 321 families here? He'd actually thought he'd get to spend some time with Susannah today. He'd be lucky if he even saw her.

That thought fell away as he fastened his work belt around his waist and hurried toward the construction area. Though the sun had barely peeked over the horizon, the sound of hammers striking nails rang out and the south wall of the structure was already taking shape. He glanced over to the long string of picnic tables near the house.

The women made quite an image, reminding him of worker bees. They were wearing gray, blue, pink, peach, even green frocks—though everyone's head was covered with the same white *kapp*. There looked to be a hundred or more of them there, many holding babies on their hips and ranging in age from the infants to an old woman he passed, who had to be a hundred if she was a day.

The concerns of the previous week fell away.

He forgot about the meetings he was required to attend with Susannah's father.

He stopped worrying about the many ways that he managed to disappoint his *daddi*.

And maybe for the first time, he let go of his wish to be in Maine.

Micah checked in with the master engineer, who assigned him to the west wall that was just being laid out. The foundation had been poured two weeks earlier. Lumber and hardware had been delivered beforehand as well, and sat waiting to be used in large organized stacks. He passed a group of men sawing floor joists to length. A group of *youngies* would carry the measured and cut boards to men standing on the foundation. Micah suspected that given the amount of workers they had, the frame, including the roof beams, would be in place well before lunch.

Soon he was intent on his section—finishing out

the frame and finding a rhythm with the large group of men in his section. Someone started singing, and soon his voice was joined by another and another. Micah became totally focused on the hammer, the nail, the song and the rising sun warming his back. He didn't realize that sweat had drenched his shirt until one of the young boys walked up with a tray of cups and water. He took two, pouring one over his neck and downing the other.

Then the second master engineer was calling out that it was time to begin the actual construction of the wall. The boards were measured and cut. Micah scrambled to the top with a dozen other men as others from the ground lifted the boards into place. The planks were positioned vertically—Micah hammered from the top as a younger guy he didn't know hammered from the bottom.

An hour later, he was once again being offered water. As he gulped it down, he looked around the roof area where he was working. An old man with white hair stood on his left and a young teen on his right. Both reflected the same grin that he felt on his own face.

And then they were working again. Micah straddled a beam so that he could nail from the outside. He looked down and counted four others doing the same. They must look like a ladder of Amish men.

He had no idea how much time had passed when he climbed down and stepped back, trying to take in the whole of what they'd done. "It's like building a house of cards," he murmured.

"Pretty much," the old guy to his right agreed, grinning and straightening his suspenders. "Much sturdier, though."

Soon they were both back on the roof again. The morning passed without Micah even being aware of it.

When he heard the lunch bell ring, he scrambled down to the ground, but then he stood there as the tide of workers swept past him. He stared up at the frame of the barn, which was now completely intact.

It really was amazing what could be done when people worked together.

Almost without realizing what he was doing, he slipped his cell phone from his back pocket and took a selfie with the barn rising behind him. Only when he touched the photo button and heard the click did he realize that what he was doing was generally frowned upon. So he stuck his phone back in his pocket and strode off toward lunch.

He'd put it on Snapchat later that evening.

One picture wouldn't hurt anything.

And it wasn't like anyone else in the group had a phone or a Snapchat account. What they didn't know wouldn't hurt them, and it wouldn't land him in trouble, either.

Or, at least, that was his thinking at the moment.

He spied Susannah twice during lunch. Both times he tried to catch her attention, but she didn't see him. Or at least she pretended not to see him.

Was she upset about the meetings they had to attend with her *dat*? He tried to remember if they'd talked about it, but she had been curiously absent when he'd worked in her *dat*'s farrier shop. He'd thought she was simply busy, but maybe she was avoiding him.

He didn't have much time to dwell on it. Before he'd even cleaned his plate, men were returning to work. The afternoon passed as quickly as the morning had. By the time he climbed down from the roof, he was sore in a way that he hadn't been in a very long time. He supposed that farming and shoeing horses didn't use the same muscles as construction. It wasn't that he was getting older. His age had nothing to do with it.

He looked for Susannah as he made his way to fetch the buggy for his grandparents. When he asked Elias, who was once again helping folks with their buggies, he learned that the Beiler family had already left.

Possibly she was avoiding him. So what? Maybe she'd decided that being his sidekick was too risky. The thought depressed him terribly. Hadn't they had fun? Hadn't she enjoyed the evening in the park and the time they'd gone fishing?

He knew she had. She'd laughed and smiled and the serious Susannah had slipped away.

But he didn't doubt that she was making an effort not to spend time with him, which was fine. He'd see her on Sunday. They had the church meeting, and there was no way she could avoid him there.

Fortunately for Susannah, Sunday morning dawned dark and rainy. She could volunteer to stay inside with the babies after service. Then she wouldn't have to deal with Micah.

So she was pretty surprised when she was sitting with Deborah, rocking babies in the Gleichs' front living room, and Micah stepped inside.

"Uh-oh. Looks like someone found you," Deborah said under her breath.

If he felt uncomfortable in a room full of babies, Micah didn't show it. But then was he ever uncomfortable? That was part of his problem—even places where he didn't belong, he still seemed to enjoy. No, that wasn't quite right. Micah Fisher was a man intent on savoring every single moment of a day, and she couldn't really blame him for that. She admired it in one way, but then there was her *dat* to think about...

"Deborah, Susannah. *Gut* to see you both."

"Is there something we can help you with, Micah?" Deborah smiled sweetly and nodded to the fussy baby in her lap. "Or maybe you had an urge to rock a *boppli*."

"I could if you need me to, not that I have any experience. I somehow managed to avoid babysitting my nieces and nephews when they were still infants. Come to think of it, I don't think I've ever—"

Deborah stood and held the crying infant out to him. "Jeremiah is teething and none too happy about it. Maybe he'll respond better to a man. And here's his Binky, which he won't take from me, and also his blanket."

And with an obvious wink at Susannah, Deborah picked up her giant purse and fled the room.

"That was embarrassing," Susannah muttered.

"What was embarrassing, and how do I get this kid to stop crying?"

"First of all, stop holding him at arm's length as if he's a fish you just caught."

"Oh."

"Closer. Snuggle him like you would a newborn."

"I don't know how to snuggle a newborn."

"Okay. First, sit down." She'd been rocking Mary Lynn, a sweet six-week-old whose *mamm* looked as if she was going to fall asleep on her feet. Susannah laid the child in a playpen that had been set up in the corner of the room, covered her with a blanket and then returned to Micah's side.

He was staring at Jeremiah as if he'd never seen a crying baby before. As for Jeremiah, his cries had reached a fever pitch.

"Sit."

"Here?"

"Sit and rock. I'll fetch a bottle."

When she returned to the room, it was quiet. Micah had the baby lying on his belly across his knees and was rubbing his back.

"Huh."

"*Huh*, what? Did you think I didn't know how to quiet a baby?"

"Quite obviously, you didn't. You said as much when you walked in."

"True, but I tried this once with a puppy I found that seemed miserable. I think he'd eaten some hamburger that had gone rancid…"

"Please don't tell me any more."

"The thing had vomited once, and he started howling. Mutt looked so pitiful that I finally went to the front porch and put him across my knees, just like this. And it worked, just like with…" He stared quizzically down at the child.

"Jeremiah."

"*Ya*. Anyway, I've been looking for you."

"Have you, now?" Baby Hannah was happily lying on her back on an old quilt and trying to catch her toes, but Susannah picked her up anyway. She suddenly needed something to do with her hands.

"Come on. Out with it. You're avoiding me."

"Why would you say that?"

"Because it's obvious you are. What gives?"

Susannah sighed. There was simply no avoiding difficult conversations with Micah. He was too direct.

"I've never been called in by my *dat* before."

"I figured as much."

"And I didn't like it one bit. Plus, I'm ashamed that I embarrassed him."

"You didn't embarrass him. I don't think he even really cared. It was that old guy, Atlee, who was stirring up trouble."

"I'm the bishop's *doschder*, Micah."

"And that means you can't have any fun?"

"That means I'm held to a higher standard."

"Sounds like pride to me. Didn't we learn at our meeting on Monday that pride is a sin?"

"Now you're mocking me."

"*Nein*, I'm not."

Baby Jeremiah had fallen asleep, and apparently Micah's knees had, too. He raised the baby to his shoulder, trying to mirror the way that Susannah was holding Hannah. It was such a funny sight, Micah juggling a baby and a blanket and a pacifier, that Susannah had trouble hanging on to her anger.

Anger.

The sermon that morning had been on anger. *The wrath of man does not work the righteousness of God.*

Susannah sighed. It seemed that in matters of Micah, whether she turned left or right, she was facing some sort of dilemma.

"I'm sorry we got in trouble about the picnic and the fishing, but as your *dat* said, it wasn't that we did anything wrong, only that we weren't thinking of how it might be viewed by others."

"So you were listening."

"Of course I was listening. I like your *dat*."

Which made her smile. He said it so simply, as if it were an obvious fact. "I like him, too."

"So would you like to go a movie next week?"

"Uh-uh. No way."

"It's a cartoon. Nothing at all racy about it."

"I'm not going to the movies."

"So you're setting me free to ask someone else? Our deal... It's over?" He smiled slyly at her. "Because I think your friend Deborah might have a thing for me."

"That is ridiculous."

"Is not."

"She left the room as soon as you walked in."

"So she's a little shy."

He was incorrigible. But then again, she had agreed to be his sidekick for as long as he was here. Come to think of it, how much longer was he going to be in Goshen?

"Any news on your moving back to Maine?"

"Now you're trying to get rid of me?"

"I did not say that."

Micah's laugh was sincere and hearty. It came from somewhere deep down in his belly. She'd never met anyone as good-natured as he was. In fact, if she were honest, Micah Fisher was a complete mystery to her.

Tuesday morning Micah still felt like he was in something of a funk. He hadn't been too surprised when Susannah turned him down for going to the movies. It wasn't forbidden, as long as they attended something G-rated or possibly PG, depending on the story. While it was true that most Amish folk didn't waste money on things like movies, it was understood that *youngies* needed to be away from the farm occasionally.

But he'd known before he asked that Susannah

wouldn't go. He'd paid attention to her reaction when her *dat* and Atlee had first called them in for The Lecture. That was how he thought about it—with capital letters. It wasn't his first reprimand and probably wouldn't be his last, but it was Susannah's first. There was no doubt about that.

She'd gone instantly rigid.

Sure, she had supported him, but as the meeting had worn on, her shoulders had tensed and she'd clasped her hands so hard that he was afraid she was going to cut off the circulation.

And then in the days immediately following, she'd started avoiding him.

The plan was for them to meet with Thomas every Monday, which they had done twice now. It hadn't been as terrible as Micah had feared. They'd discussed the *Ordnung* in general, events they were looking forward to and how they were feeling about their circumstances. Micah wasn't big on talking about feelings—he had them, same as everyone else. But what was the point in dwelling on them?

Did he feel like he'd been cast out from his home? Yes.

Did he struggle against the restrictions of the *Ordnung*? Yes!

Did he wish to remain Amish? Well, yes, of course he did. He simply didn't understand why it had to be so difficult and confining.

And so, he dithered. That was the only word for it and one his grandmother used—in fact, she'd accused him of that very thing just the day before. *Micah, I love you more than the breath in my lungs, but you can dither more than any man or child I've ever met.* He'd waited until he was in the barn brushing down the buggy horse to look up the meaning on his phone.

Webster's online claimed it meant to be indecisive.

Well, the fact that he was standing in a horse stall using his cell phone pretty much confirmed that he was indecisive—at least about whether to join the church and commit to following the rules of the *Ordnung* for the rest of his life. Moreover, he didn't see why he had to make a decision now. What was the rush? He probably had sixty years stretching in front of him. There was plenty of time to settle down and be a good Amish person.

In the days immediately following The Lecture, he'd told himself none of this mattered.

He often found himself once again calculating the date until his six months was up, but just looking at the days on the calendar filled him with dread. The immense amount of time that was left before he could even think about returning home, the idea of working every morning in the field and every afternoon in the farrier shop, the fact that he and Susannah hadn't done anything fun in nearly ten days…it all depressed him.

On the Tuesday after he'd talked to her in the nursery, he decided he might go crazy if he didn't take a few hours off from the farm. Fortunately, he'd finished up in the farrier shop early. Thomas was having a business meeting with the other members of church leadership—something about the benevolence fund. Micah had the afternoon free, and he'd seen on his phone that the sports store in town was having a clearance sale.

Few things cheered him up like a new hunting rifle or crossbow or fishing gear. His home town of Smyrna was located in the northeastern part of Maine, and was well-known for its fishing opportunities—whitefish, three kinds of trout and two kinds of bass. Just thinking about the fall fishing cheered him up, and he did have a little extra money in his pocket from working for Thomas. Certainly it wouldn't hurt to spend part of it, and he could stop by Jo Jo's Pretzels for a snack afterward.

The thought of a few hours in town had him humming to himself. As he cleaned up and shelved the tools in Thomas's shop, it occurred to him that the only thing that would make his plan better would be if Susannah went along with him. Not that he thought of her in any romantic way—she'd made it quite clear that she wasn't interested in dating—but the girl needed some relaxation time.

Whistling as he walked across the yard, he stuck his head into Susannah's sewing shop, but the place was empty. In fact, it was terribly neat, as if she hadn't been there all day. He started to climb the steps to knock on the front door, but he didn't want to wake the twins if they were napping. They probably weren't, but since it was so quiet, they might be.

Then again, maybe Susannah was around back, working in the garden. He walked down the steps of the porch, around the house, and stopped short when he saw her sitting on the bench next to the garden.

She was sitting in the sun, her head back and her eyes closed. Something caught in Micah's throat. Susannah was a beautiful woman, and she didn't seem to be aware of that fact at all. But it wasn't that awareness that caused him to stand perfectly still staring at her.

She must have washed her hair and was drying it in the sun. Her *kapp* lay on the bench beside her, and as he watched, she reached up a hand to run it through her hair—her beautiful, short brown hair. Then, as if she sensed him there, she turned to look at him. Her eyes widened, and Micah knew that there was no backing out of the situation. So instead he did what he always did: he plunged forward.

It would seem that Susannah had secrets of her own, and he was about to find out exactly what and why she'd been keeping them from him.

He strode over to where she was sitting and straddled the bench. He didn't say anything, deciding to let her lead the conversation, but it was hard to just sit there and wait. He had an overwhelming urge to reach out and run his fingers through her hair. He could see now that it only fell an inch past her ears. The look was so incongruous—an Amish woman with bobbed hair—that he honestly didn't know what to say.

When he'd waited as long as he could, he finally stated the obvious, "Must be hair-washing day."

"Ya."

Maybe it was the way she looked up shyly at him, but Micah could no longer resist. He reached out and ran his hand over the top of her head, trailing the golden brown strands to her neck. Her hair felt like silk in his fingers. He wanted to run his fingers through it, but he knew that would be inappropriate, so instead he crossed his arms and said, "Short hair looks *gut* on you."

"That's it?"

"What?"

"That's all you're going to say?"

Micah shrugged, doing his best to look nonchalant. "I suppose there's a story there, but if you wanted to tell me, you would."

"Astute."

"I am all ears, if you have an urge to share. Finished

my work in the shop, cleaned up everything and was just…you know…hanging out."

"You want to go somewhere."

"Maybe."

"And you don't want to go alone."

"I go places alone."

Susannah's grin spread, but then she spied her *kapp* sitting between them and snatched it off the bench.

"Your hair's almost dry."

"Doesn't take very long, not like when I was younger."

And then, he did what he'd told himself he wasn't going to do—he asked.

"Why's your hair short, Susannah? I'm the renegade here, so I know you didn't cut it because of a dare or a wild urge."

"*Nein.* Nothing like that."

"You don't have to explain if you don't want to."

A look of vulnerability crossed her features. Her customary mask—the one that said she knew what the answers were and had no doubt how things would turn out—slipped. Then a bird called out from a neighboring bush, broke the spell and the proper Susannah was back.

"It's not such a mystery, and honestly I didn't know that you didn't know. Maybe I did realize you didn't know, but then it seemed awkward to bring it up."

"What don't I know?"

She looked left, then right, then out across the garden. When he didn't rescue her from the discomfort of the moment, she met his gaze and said simply, "I had cancer."

It was the very last words he would have expected to come out of her mouth.

"What? When?"

"Diagnosed two years ago, just before my twenty-third birthday. We didn't catch it early enough, so I had chemo before and after the surgery."

"Chemo?"

"*Ya*. It caused my hair to fall out." She ran a hand over the top of her head, as if she needed to assure herself it was no longer bald. "It's growing back quicker than I thought."

Her voice had dropped to a whisper. "Soon no one will be able to tell."

"Who cares about your hair?" The words came out more abruptly than he'd intended. "What I mean is, your hair looks *gut* that way, but more important, how are you? Are you still sick? And why did you never tell me this?"

"Why would I tell you?"

"Because we're friends!" Micah wanted to jump up and pace back and forth, but he forced himself to remain seated. When Susannah still didn't look at him, he put a hand on each of her shoulders and waited until she finally raised her gaze to his. "We're friends. Right?"

"*Ya*. Of course."

"So tell me about this. How do you feel? Will you need more surgery or more chemo? And what is your prognosis?"

"Fine, probably not and *gut*."

Micah let his hands fall to his side. There was something about the way that Susannah was looking at him that made him squirm. As if she were waiting for him to figure it out. But figure what out?

Then it occurred to him. Like a bolt of lightning illuminating a dark night, his mind put the pieces of Susannah's puzzle together.

"This is why you don't date?"

Susannah became suddenly interested in the dirt under her thumbnail. "Maybe. I guess."

"That's ridiculous."

"How would you know?"

"Because it doesn't matter."

"It does matter."

"No, what matters is what type of person you are and whether you have feelings for someone—not that you had cancer and are now in recovery."

Susannah tapped a finger against her lips. Her eyebrows were pulled down into a V, and her eyes seemed to be glistening. Was she going to cry?

"I can't have children, Micah."

"What?"

"Because of the type of cancer I had, I can't have children."

"What does that have to do with anything? Why would that make you decide to stop dating?"

"Because there's no point."

"No point?"

She looked at him directly now, her chin up and her eyes daring him to argue with her. "We both know what that means to an Amish family, to an Amish man. Sure, I dated before my diagnosis, but now I understand—"

He cut her off, his impatience suddenly overpowering his vow to let her tell the story in her own way.

"You understand what exactly? That no one would want you? Because that's foolish and… Well, it's wrong."

"Is it?"

"Yes!"

"I don't exactly have men lining up at the door."

"Maybe because you keep everyone at arm's length."

"Or maybe because they would want children." Her anger was winning out over her embarrassment.

Micah was almost relieved to see the return of the Susannah he'd come to know—obstinate and strong-willed, sure, but not heartbroken. One more minute of the heartbroken Susannah, and he would have pulled her into his arms and embarrassed them both.

"Not all men want *kinner*."

"All Amish men do. Trust me, I know."

She leaned her neck forward, twisted her hair into some sort of knot and then secured it with bobby pins that were lying on the bench. How did women do that? He couldn't brush his own teeth without looking in a mirror.

She adjusted the *kapp* on her head, then turned and stared at him, as if she was daring him to push further.

Fine.

He'd push.

Because Susannah needed to realize that any man would be lucky to have her as a *fraa*, children or no children.

"Not everyone wants children, Susannah. You can't not date because of that."

"Of course I can, and that's a personal decision, thank you very much."

"So what do you see as your future? Living with your parents the rest of your life? Hiding in your sewing room and making quilts for other families because you don't deserve to have one?"

He knew he'd hit a nerve by the way she catapulted off the bench.

"I'll thank you to keep your nose out of my future."

"Oh, really? Because you're pretty intent on sticking your nose in mine."

"I have been trying to be your friend."

"You've been trying to corral me, to keep me away from anyone in this stupid town, to keep your girlfriends safe from me as if I'm some kind of ogre that might corrupt them."

But Susannah wasn't listening to him anymore. She was storming away as if they were an old married couple having a fight. He didn't know if he should follow her or not, but by the time he made up his mind that he should, she'd gone into the house and slammed the door quite forcefully behind her.

Which pretty much ended any conversation they were having.

Chapter Six

"You haven't talked to him in two days?" Deborah yanked on the yarn she was knitting with. It was a pastel color and self-striping. She was making a baby blanket for her *schweschder*. Someone in Deborah's family was always about to have a baby. It was a good thing that she was a fast knitter.

Susannah had stopped by to drop off some hot pads and aprons she'd made from fabric scraps. Deborah's family had a good-sized produce shed where they sold everything from fresh vegetables to eggs to knitted items. Susannah kept a corner table filled with quilts, pot holders, aprons, even table runners. Though she offered to work one day a week at the shed, Deborah's parents insisted there was no need. They had twelve children, so there was always someone willing and able to work a few hours.

She'd brought along an infant quilt that she was hand sewing the binding to. As she knotted her thread and pulled it through the back of the quilt, she tried to think how best to answer Deborah's question.

"It's a simple yes or no."

"Yes. We haven't spoken since Tuesday."

"Because you're embarrassed?"

"I don't know. Maybe?"

"Why would you be embarrassed, Susannah? It's not like you dyed your hair pink."

"Indeed."

"Anyway, I think I know what's really going on here."

"Oh, you do, do you?"

"It's so obvious." Deborah waved a knitting needle at her and then stuck it back into her next stitch and tugged again on the ball of yarn. "You have a crush on Micah Fisher."

"I do not!"

"I think you do."

"And I think you've been staring at that ball of yarn too long, because you're sounding a little crazy."

"You don't want him dating anyone else."

"Of course I don't. He's trouble wrapped up in suspenders."

"Okay. That sounded plausible when you first told me of your plan to tag along with him. I even admired you for sacrificing your free time to keep him in check."

"I do not keep him in check. Trust me on that."

"Many in our community were perhaps too quick to believe the rumors about Micah, and I'm embarrassed to admit that I might have been one of them. You have to admit that he is…different."

"Oh, I'm aware of that."

"Does he still have the phone?"

"Of course."

"Still wearing *Englisch* clothes?"

"He occasionally swaps out his straw hat for his baseball cap."

"But none of those are actual crimes." Deborah finished the row she was knitting and turned the blanket to purl in the opposite direction. "After he first arrived, when he was sneaking out of his own house, I thought he wouldn't last more than a week."

"The trouble he does manage to get into is so..." Susannah stared down at the needle and thread in her hand, trying to remember what she was doing with it. "Trivial. That's what it is—trivial. Silly stuff."

Deborah stopped knitting and waited for Susannah to look up at her. Lowering her voice, as if she could cushion the blow, she asked, "Did you hear about his picture in the paper?"

"What?"

Deborah reached down into her large purse. She pulled out a paperback book, what looked like a sandwich wrapped in wax paper, a bottle of water and a tube of hand lotion.

"Doesn't that bag hurt your shoulder?"

"Mostly it sits on the ground."

"I still don't understand why you carry so much around."

"If you had eleven siblings, you'd understand."

"I suppose."

"Here it is." Instead of looking pleased with herself, Deborah's expression said that she wanted to apologize. She didn't, though. Without saying another word, she handed a copy of the local newspaper to Susannah.

"Why would I want to read about the city's contract for a new water tower?"

"Not there." Deborah reached over and flipped the paper so that Susannah could read below the fold. "There."

Susannah actually felt light-headed as she stared down at the photo of Micah standing in front of the barn that was only partially completed. He was wearing his usual cocky smile. In the background it was plain to see several other Amish workers picking up tools or climbing down from the roof. If she guessed, Susannah would say he'd taken it as they were breaking for lunch.

"I can't… I can't believe he'd do this."

"Trivial, as you say, and yet plenty of folks in our community are upset about it."

"Why did you wait so long to show it to me?"

"You've only been here a half hour."

"Still, I would think you'd have pulled it out as soon as I climbed down from my buggy."

"I'm not any happier about this than you are." Deborah resumed knitting. "I don't like being the bearer of bad news."

"I just… I can't believe Micah would do this. He submitted it for photo of the week?" As she continued reading, her mouth dropped open in disbelief. "He won fifty dollars?"

"So it says."

"He doesn't even need the money. I know he's making plenty from my *dat*, and besides, he rarely has time to spend it, since he's working for his *daddi* in the mornings and with the horses in the afternoon."

"It wonders me."

Susannah refolded the paper and held it out to Deborah.

"I'm sorry," Deborah said.

"For what?"

"Ruining your day."

"I'm glad you showed me." Susannah stared down at the paper that they were now both holding, then she jerked it back. "Maybe I should keep it, if that's all right with you."

"Sure. Of course."

Susannah set the offending newsprint down next to her purse. She tried to focus on the quilt in her hands. Sewing always relaxed her. It was immensely satisfying to see random pieces of fabric become something that would warm or comfort another person—often a person she didn't even know. She slipped her needle into the binding of the quilt, pulled it through, then slipped it into the quilt itself. The ladder stitch was one of her favorites, invisibly closing the two seams together. If only life were so easily patched.

Deborah cleared her throat. "So, about your crush…"

"I do not have a crush on Micah."

"Then why did you wait so long to tell him about your cancer? Why did you wait until he stumbled over the fact?"

"I don't know, honestly. I thought about telling him—a few times. But always it seemed like such a downer, or like I would be asking for sympathy."

Instead of answering, Deborah raised an eyebrow and motioned for her to continue.

"And I didn't want his sympathy. You have no idea how tiresome it is to have people pat you on the hand and ask 'how are you getting along, dear?' in that syrupy-sweet voice."

"They mean well, I'm sure."

"Of course they do, but I'm not fragile. I'm not going to break in two simply because I had cancer. In fact, you know what?" She tugged three more stitches through the binding, tacked down the corner and then stowed her needle by rocking it through both layers of fabric. "I do like being around Micah, or I did, because he didn't know about my cancer. He treated me like he would any other woman."

"Ah."

"Ah? That's your response? Ah?" Susannah realized in that moment that she'd been avoiding examining her feelings toward Micah. Was she afraid that she was falling for him? That was ridiculous. Micah Fisher was not her type, and even if he was, he wasn't staying in Goshen. Still, there was something about him that she'd never encountered before in the few men she'd dated.

"What response did you expect?"

"I don't know. I thought you might understand. You know how it was when I first found out."

"I'm the first person you told."

"And then when Samuel broke up with me."

"He didn't deserve you. By the way, I heard that girl from Shipshe he was dating dumped him."

There was a time when news of Samuel caused her heart to twist, but Susannah realized she wasn't really interested in his dating life. Sometime between their breakup and now, she had moved on.

"I never felt around Samuel like I do around Micah."

"Oh, my. That sounds serious."

"*Nein.* It's not like that. I keep telling you. It's less like when you have a crush on someone and more like I can be myself. Not Cancer Survivor Susannah but... just Susannah."

"I suppose it makes sense."

"What does?"

"This strange attraction you two have, and don't deny that he likes being around you, too. It's plain as day to anyone with eyes and a brain."

Susannah folded her quilt, stuffed it into her sewing bag and sat back in the lawn chair. "Please explain."

"Micah is attracted to you—"

"He is not."

"He touched your hair."

"Whatever. Probably he was in shock. Go on."

"Micah is attracted to you because you're not a risk taker. You're a rule follower. You're the ultimate challenge to a guy like him."

Susannah felt an irrational urge to cover her ears, and yet, didn't she want to hear her friend's opinion? Deborah had always been the one person who would be completely honest with her. Even during her illness, when she was bald and exhausted and looked terrible, Deborah had been refreshingly candid. Instead of claiming she looked fine, Deborah had suggested they add color to her wardrobe. Then she'd proceeded to knit incredibly soft hats and scarfs in blues and greens and lavender, claiming the color gave her a healthier glow.

Susannah didn't know if it had helped her glow. She'd never really thought of herself as a glowing type of person. But the small gifts definitely lifted her spirits, that and the fact that her friend had been honest with her.

"You're an attractive woman, Susannah. And it's not prideful for me to say that about you. It's only prideful for you to think it of yourself." Deborah paused, stared out at the tables laden with goods to sell and then glanced back at Susannah, a smile tugging at the corners of her mouth. "Or maybe pride isn't involved at all. Maybe it's just an observation."

"Danki."

"Where was I?"

"You were explaining why Micah is attracted to me, something that I have to tell you I don't see at all."

"What about the night you were fishing, when you thought he was going to kiss you?"

"I should never have told you that."

Deborah frowned down at her knitting, paused to count her stitches, placed a marker and resumed working on the row. "We've been telling each other about first kisses since we were fourteen."

"You and Josiah behind the schoolhouse."

"Uh-huh." Deborah grinned at the memory. "As I said earlier, I think maybe you and Micah started out as enemies…"

"Scripture reminds us to have an attitude of kindness to all."

"Then whatever you felt for one another moved to friendship when you began to understand each other."

"We're also called to be friends to one another—love your neighbor as yourself."

"And now it's blossoming into something more than mere friendship." Deborah focused on the row she was knitting with a flourish of needles and waited.

Susannah had no idea what to say. Was it possible that Deborah was right?

"Comments? Insights? Objections?"

Susannah felt an unexpected release of the tension she'd been carrying around for some time. Her shoulders relaxed and the headache that had been teasing her all morning dissipated. She had the sense that she was letting go of something that she'd been holding on to for a long while, perhaps since she'd first talked to Micah standing in the road leading to their respective houses.

"It could be you're right. I'm not saying you are, but I

will say that I feel…confused. Some days I do find my-self thinking that Micah would make a fine husband, and yes, occasionally I drift off into daydreams about that."

Deborah smiled, but she didn't interrupt, and she certainly didn't say the four dreaded words: *I told you so.*

"I realize how silly that is. He's not even staying here in Indiana. If you could hear him go on and on about Maine."

"I have. We all have." Deborah set aside her knitting, walked over in front of Susannah's chair and squatted in front of her. "It's okay to enjoy this time with Micah."

"It is? But—"

Deborah put her hands over Susannah's. "Maybe it will lead to something else and maybe it won't. All we know for certain is that *Gotte* brought you two together during this time in your lives for a reason."

"But I have no idea what that reason is."

"That's okay."

"Then what am I supposed to do?"

"How about you do the simplest of things? Just savor it and stop worrying about where it might or might not lead."

Micah nearly swallowed his gum when Susannah walked into his *daddi*'s barn early that evening.

"I thought you weren't talking to me."

"Why would you think that?"

"Because you walked away."

"Oh, yeah. I did."

"Not that I blame you. I overstepped. I tried to lecture you on your life when my own life is a mess."

Instead of denying that, she simply said, "I might have overreacted."

Which was all the apology he was going to get. But then, maybe she didn't owe him an apology. Maybe he owed her one. Regardless, Susannah seemed to have moved on.

Micah had been oiling and mending one of the harnesses. He set it aside and studied her as she stood there in the doorway to the barn, the last of the day's light splashing over her. She was a sight for sore eyes, that was for certain. He'd tossed and turned until midnight the previous evening, wondering how he was going to survive the remainder of his Indiana exile without Susannah by his side.

"My parents used to have tiffs," he admitted.

"Did they, now?"

"Couple of times a year. Nothing terrible, just a bit of a row and then an awkward silence for the remainder of the day."

Susannah looked intrigued. "My parents never fight, not that I'm aware of."

"Could be because my *mamm* has a temper, or because my *dat* is more stubborn than any mule you will ever encounter." He walked past her, out into the fading sunshine. Watching the sun set in the west, looking out over the fields, he realized that Indiana had a certain unique beauty. Not that it could compare with Maine, and not that he'd ever want to live here, but he could understand why people did. "It used to upset me when I was a *youngie*."

"What did you do?"

"What most Amish *kinner* do. I ran to my grandparents. This would be my *mamm*'s parents. They moved up to join us in Maine after the first year. You'd think that they would be on her side."

"They weren't?"

Micah shrugged. "Couldn't ever tell, but I do remember what my *daddi* said to me after one particularly loud argument my parents had. I was sitting out near the pond, but not fishing. He came over and told me not to worry. He said if my parents were perfect, they wouldn't have married each other. But since neither one was perfect, I could rest assured that they would forgive each other."

Susannah started laughing, and then Micah started laughing, and then he knew that everything was okay between them. They both sat on the bench under the barn's overhang.

Susannah bumped her shoulder against his. "No perfect people in your family, huh?"

"Not a single one."

"Mine, either."

"Which, I suppose, means we're not perfect."

"Not even close." Susannah pulled a folded sheet of newspaper from her pocket. "And now that we've established that neither of us is perfect, we should probably talk about this."

Micah stared at it, dumbfounded for the space of a few seconds. Then he hopped up, walked across the barn and retrieved his phone from the shelf where he usually stored it. He returned to where Susannah was and attempted to turn it on, but nothing happened.

"Problem?"

"It's dead."

"Ah."

"I don't think I've even used it since the workday at the barn." He waited, expecting her to begin scolding him for using it at all. When she didn't, he sat back down beside her. "There was a time when I checked it every day. Who am I fooling? I checked it every hour. I thought... Well, I guess I thought I was going to miss out on something."

"How so?"

"Well, I have *freinden* on different chat apps."

"Real friends?"

Micah shrugged his shoulder. "They seemed to be at the time, and maybe they were. Or they could have been, if our lives had connected in a more tangible way. I don't know. At the time that I bought this phone, I was feeling like no one understood me. And suddenly there was this virtual community where people did understand. It was nice."

"And now?"

"Now I don't know if any of what goes on through this device is real."

He scrubbed a hand over his face. "If I were to be honest? Now I would rather spend time with you and Deborah and even her *bruder* Elias."

"I didn't know you'd spent any time with Elias."

Micah didn't try to explain that Elias was okay but he enjoyed his time with Susannah more. He didn't know how to say that without making a fool of himself. As he mulled over that fact, Susannah studied him, and he almost fell over when she started laughing.

"Are you sure you're feeling all right?" he asked. "You're acting a little odd."

"It just occurred to me that your chat apps aren't so very different from the *Englisch* pen pal that I have."

"Now you're just tugging on my suspenders."

"*Nein.* It's true."

"How did Susannah Beiler, bishop's *doschder*, end up with an *Englisch* pen pal?"

"Jayla was in the hospital when I was... We shared a room for a while."

"Did she have cancer, too?"

"*She did.* She's older than me by a few years, African

American and already had one *boppli*. We're as different as two people can be."

"Like me and my *freinden* on Snapchat."

"Maybe, which I guess is part of what I like about writing to her. She helps me to see my life from a different perspective."

"And you still exchange letters?"

"We do. We've even met up for coffee a couple of times, when she was back in town for treatment. She lives over by Millersburg, so it doesn't happen as often as I'd like, but I always look forward to seeing her. And her letters—it cheers me up just to see her return address on an envelope." Susannah reached out and poked his phone with a finger. "So, how were you going to learn more about the picture you took from the phone?"

"I was just going to check and see if I could figure out how this happened." He picked up the paper again and stared at it, as if doing so would make the puzzle pieces fall together.

Finally, he handed it back to her. "I don't know how that photo ended up in the paper."

"But you took it?"

"*Ya*. Plainly it's a selfie that I snapped. I even remember taking it. I was thinking I'd like to show it to my family when I get back to Maine."

"Why?" There was no condemnation in her voice, only curiosity. "Surely you have barn raisings in Maine."

Micah was shaking his head before she even finished. "Not like here. That…" He nodded toward the paper she was now holding. "That was a completely different experience for me. In Maine, our communities are much smaller."

"You still help one another."

"Of course, but a barn isn't raised in a day. We might have one big workday at the beginning, but the majority of the work is done as people are able over the period of a week or two." He stood, paced back and forth in front of her for a minute and finally leaned against the barn post, crossing his arms. "I don't know how that picture ended up in the paper, and I know nothing about winning fifty dollars."

"But you think you can figure that out through your phone?"

"Maybe."

Susannah stood and straightened her apron, then stepped closer and smiled up at him. "Perhaps we should go to town tomorrow."

"Town?"

"I heard Dairy Queen has a special on their ice cream."

"Do they, now?"

"Personally, I could go for something cold and chocolate."

"I could probably charge my phone while we're there."

"Exactly."

"What time should I pick you up?"

"We can go whenever you finish your work with my *dat*."

Micah couldn't believe how much his mood had lifted since she'd stepped into the barn. Did Susannah's opinion of him matter so much? And why wasn't she more angry about the picture? She was always lecturing him about staying within the guidelines of the *Ordnung*, but she hadn't said a word about it since arriving. He knew that asking her wouldn't yield answers, and maybe the *why* didn't matter so much after all.

When she'd arrived, the sun was just beginning to set, but while they'd talked, twilight had crept over the fields.

"Let me hop inside and tell my grandparents that I'm going to walk you home."

"I'm pretty sure I can find my way."

"Still…" And rather than explain, he jogged toward the house, returning in a few minutes with a flashlight, a napkin filled with a few of his *mammi*'s brownies and a quart jar full of milk.

"Didn't expect you to bring a picnic."

"Just thought you might like something sweet."

They stopped at the top of the small hill that sat just inside the boundary line on her parents' property. Susannah was wearing a sweater, and Micah had on a jacket. He slipped it off and put it on the ground for her to sit on.

"Seriously?"

"Wouldn't want you to get your dress…" And then words seemed to fail him as he looked at her in the soft light of the moon. The stars shone as if they'd been flung there particularly for the two of them. He thought of kissing her, then wondered why he'd even have such a thought and then wondered if she'd want him to. Finally, he thrust the brownies at her. "Hope you like walnuts."

"I love walnuts."

They didn't speak again until they'd finished the snack. Passing the quart jar back and forth felt curiously intimate. The brownies were still warm, the milk cold and the sky above them offered a spectacular canopy of the heavens.

He didn't want to push, didn't want to spook her away again, but he wanted to know. For some reason he couldn't put his finger on, he needed to know. And since she didn't seem in a rush to get home, now was as good a time as any. Now might be the best chance he'd get. So he crossed his legs at the ankle, leaned back on his hands and asked what he'd wanted to ask since the day he'd walked up on her drying her short hair in the sun.

"What was it like?"

"Cancer?"

"Being afraid that you might die. How did you get past that every day?"

"I guess during those first few weeks, I was just in shock."

"You didn't realize something was wrong before your diagnosis?"

"Not initially. I became worried when I started losing weight, had trouble eating and then there was the pain." She placed a hand on her stomach.

When she didn't continue, Micah reached for her hand and entwined their fingers together.

"And you had surgery?"

"Ya." Her voice was a whisper, practically a caress.

"That must have been frightening."

"The diagnosis was probably the worst part. After that, it was simply a matter of weighing my options. And my parents were very supportive for whatever I wanted to do."

"Did you have options? Other than the surgery?"

"Not really. But if I'd said I needed time, if I'd wanted to wait, my parents would have understood."

Micah stared down at their hands, which he could just barely make out in the darkness. He rubbed his thumb over hers. "I would never have guessed that you'd been sick."

"Is that so?"

"You're so spunky."

"Spunky?"

"I guess I was a little afraid of you when I first met you."

Susannah began giggling. Snatching her hand from his, she covered her mouth…until she'd worked herself up to a full belly laugh.

"Not that funny."

"It…it sort of is."

Which was followed by more laughter, and Susannah gulping for air, which started Micah to laughing, though he couldn't have said what he was laughing about.

But suddenly it didn't matter why they were laughing, sitting on top of the hill, the stars spread out before them like grains of sand on a beach.

It occurred to Micah then that he should step back. The be-careful voice in his head asked what he thought he was doing.

She's not your type, buddy.

She's out of your league.

She's the bishop's daughter, and don't forget you're heading back to Maine as soon as possible.

As they walked toward her parents' home, he realized that most people he knew would agree with that voice of reason. But when had he ever listened to reason or cared what other people thought?

Never.

And he didn't plan on starting now. He might be in trouble with her *dat* for the picture, but he suspected things would be even worse with his *daddi*. In fact, the picture on the front page of the *Goshen News* might be the final straw. Micah understood he should be worried about that, but at the moment he would rather keep his attention on the beautiful woman walking at his side.

Chapter Seven

When Susannah suggested going to town to charge Micah's phone, she had thought she could sneak away from the farm for a few hours. Normally that wouldn't have been a problem. Unfortunately, the next day her *mamm* was called to a neighbor's to help with a sick *aenti* and her *dat* was attending a monthly meeting of area bishops.

"I'm stuck with these two," she explained to Micah.

"Hey! You're not stuck with us. You love us." Sharon was sticking flower seeds into pots, though in the process, more dirt ended up on her than around the seeds.

Shiloh was sitting on the back porch step, writing her letters on a tablet. "Does this look right, Susannah?"

"Sure it does."

"I think the tail of my *g* needs to hang down more." She flipped the pencil around and began vigorously erasing.

"Those two are yin and yang." Micah sat in the rocking chair beside Susannah. He kept watching her, like he wanted to say something, but then he would look away. Perhaps he didn't want to talk in front of Sharon and Shiloh—little pitchers having big ears and all of that.

"Yin and what?"

"They're like flip sides of the same coin."

"Oh, *ya*. They look alike but often act very different."

"Which one is more like you?"

"I don't have freckles like Sharon."

"You called them stardust." Sharon put her dirty hands on her nonexistent hips and cocked her head. "Remember?"

"She has *gut* hearing."

"Yes, they both do."

Shiloh remained focused over her tablet. "I don't have freckles, either, but you said I had the stars in my eyes."

"Yes, you do, Shiloh."

"You told them that?"

Susannah's mind was spinning, trying to keep up with three conversations at once. She finally gave up and focused on Micah. "The point is that we can't go to town for ice cream."

She knew she'd made a mistake the second the words slipped out of her mouth. Her *schweschdern* might be complete opposites on some things, but at other times they merged together into one entity. This was one of those times.

"We want to go for ice cream."

"We did all our chores."

"And you promised we'd do something fun."

"And planting flowers isn't that much fun."

"And I love ice cream."

Micah looked as if he were going to burst out laughing. Fortunately, he held it in or Susannah would have been tempted to dump one of Sharon's pots of dirt over his head. Laughing at the girls convinced them they were entertaining, and from that point there was no turning back.

"We could take them with us," Micah suggested, which pretty much sealed her fate for the day. There was no stopping her twin sisters when they had another adult on their side.

Susannah insisted they walk next door with Micah while he fetched his *daddi*'s horse and buggy. "It'll wear these two out, and as you've noticed they have a lot of energy."

Sharon had repeatedly dodged ahead of them and circled back. As usual, Shiloh stuck close to Susannah's side, though at the moment she was hopping from foot to foot.

Micah's *mammi* actually clapped her hands when they walked up to the front door. "It seems I haven't seen you girls in ages."

"We're going for ice cream."

"Micah's going to take us."

"If he can borrow the buggy."

"Well, of course he can." She reached out and put a hand on both girls, ushering them into the house. "Come in. Come in. Susannah, it's been too long since you stopped by."

Soon they were settled around the kitchen table, and Micah had explained why he wanted to use the buggy. "But only if you don't need it."

Mammi smiled at the girls, then turned her attention to Micah. "I had planned to go and visit Miriam Hochstettler, who's had a flare-up of her rheumatoid arthritis."

"We can go another day."

"Nonsense. You go on out and tell your *daddi* that you need the buggy. I can visit Miriam tomorrow."

"But—"

"*Nein*. I insist. These two girls look like they've been working hard all day. They've earned a treat."

Susannah couldn't help laughing. "Sharon certainly does look as if she's been working hard. There's more dirt on her apron than in the pots of flowers she was planting."

"Nothing that won't wash out," Abigail assured her.

"And I've been writing my letters," Shiloh chimed in.

"Aren't you a smart girl."

"We have to go to school next year." Sharon's voice dropped an octave and she ducked her head. "Whether we want to or not."

Which earned a laugh all around.

Micah moved to the back door to go and bring the buggy around. As an afterthought, he turned back to Sharon and Shiloh. "Do you girls want to help me?"

He started laughing as they dashed out the back door ahead of him. "I'll take that as a *yes*."

Susannah and Abigail caught up on what was happening on both farms—which wasn't much.

Glancing at the kitchen clock, Susannah said, "I suppose I should go on out. I don't want to keep Micah waiting."

"Or the girls. They seemed quite excited."

Susannah walked with Abigail out to the front porch, where they sat and waited for Micah to bring the buggy around.

"I've been meaning to speak to you regarding Micah. We appreciate your befriending him."

"Micah's an easy person to like."

"That's what we're a little worried about."

"What I mean is that he's a hard worker and he has a *gut* attitude. Even my *dat* says so."

"I agree with both of those points, but you and I both know that Micah hasn't made up his mind on some very important life choices."

"I'm not sure what you mean."

Abigail set her rocker in motion. "Oh, I pray every day that all of my *family* will stay in the faith, but not all do. That's a truth to be reckoned with."

Susannah started to protest, but Abigail raised a hand to stop anything she might have said. "You're young yet, so it's hard for you to imagine."

"I do have *freinden* who have joined the Mennonite church."

"And it's not my place to say whether that is right or wrong. *Gotte* directs each path. However, if what I know about you and your family is correct—and we've lived next door to each other all of your life—then you have no plans to leave our church or our community."

"*Nein.* Of course not. Well, I've always thought of myself as Plain, and I suppose I will stay in Goshen. Where else would I go?"

"My point is Micah may not stay in our faith."

"He told you that?"

"His actions told me that, and you would arrive at the same conclusion if you'd get the stars out of your eyes."

Susannah sifted through her memories of time spent with Micah, searching for a way to defend herself. She finally settled for "I do not have stars in my eyes."

"Looks that way from here, and normally I would be thrilled at the thought of having you as a part of the family."

Susannah jumped to her feet at the word *family*. Fortunately, Micah pulled the buggy up in front of the porch at that moment.

"I have to go."

"Just remember what I said, Susannah, and guard your heart."

Those words bounced round and round her mind as she climbed into the buggy, made sure the girls were sitting back properly, and listened to Micah discuss a horse he had shoed that morning. Only she wasn't really hearing him.

She was thinking about Abigail Fisher warning her to guard her heart.

The day was warm, and Micah needed to charge his phone, so they ate their treats inside. Susannah and Micah sat on one side of the booth, Sharon and Shiloh sat on the other.

It took a few minutes for his cell phone to come to life. When it did, Micah started punching buttons. Sharon and Shiloh seemed not to notice. They were busy licking at the ice cream cones while at the same time coloring the place mats that the girl working the front counter had given them. Susannah glanced around the restaurant. It was plenty full for three in the afternoon.

One couple sat in a booth across from them. Their young child in a highchair was leaning forward to touch the screen of some small tablet. Across the restaurant another toddler, surely not yet walking, was crying and reaching for his *mamm*'s phone. Even the employee who was supposed to be bussing tables had pulled out his phone and was staring at it, the cluttered table in front of him temporarily forgotten.

She hadn't really paid attention to how much *Englischers* used their electronic devices. What were they looking at? What could be so fascinating? She glanced again at her *schweschdern*. They were adorable, their heads practically touching as they worked on a puzzle on the color sheet. Both were wearing white *kapps* and blue dresses with blue aprons, and for a moment Susannah realized how different they must look to *Englischers*.

She knew it wasn't her place to say who was right or wrong. Her *dat* had often reminded her *not to judge lest ye be judged*. She thought she knew what was right for her, but did that mean that other ways were wrong?

Why did there have to be a right or wrong anyway?

Some people chose to be farmers, some woodworkers. Some people were *Englisch* and others were Amish. What mattered was how they treated one another and how they lived their lives. She glanced at Micah and once again heard Abigail's words. *Guard your heart.* Was she falling in love with Micah Fisher? And even if she was, who was to say that it would end badly?

It probably would end badly.

He was definitely moving back to Maine as soon as possible.

She couldn't imagine living so far from her family, even if he did care about her in that way, which was by no means certain.

Micah turned off his phone and focused on his sundae.

"Well?"

"Well, what?"

"Did you figure it out?"

"Oh, *ya*. I figured it out."

"And?"

He looked at her and smiled as he shoveled in another rather large spoonful of ice cream. "I'm suddenly starved. I could eat two of these."

"You're suddenly avoiding the subject. Out with it."

Micah wiped his mouth with a napkin and cornered himself in the booth so that he could look directly at her. "I took the selfie and posted it to Snapchat the day of the barn raising. As I told you, I haven't even used the phone since."

"So how did it get to the paper?"

"A friend of mine—an *Englischer*—managed to capture the photograph and then he sent it into the paper, pretending to be me."

"Why would he do that?"

"I might have mentioned that I'm running a little low on money."

"My *dat* is paying you."

"*Ya*, and I give all of that money to my *daddi* as I should, since he's feeding me and providing me a place to stay. But that doesn't leave anything for..." He glanced at the girls and cleared his throat, then leaned closer and lowered his voice. "Doesn't leave anything for dating."

Susannah felt her cheeks flame red. She would have stopped it if she could, but she'd always blushed when she was embarrassed. Micah was looking at her as if she was the most important thing in the world, and he definitely noticed her sudden fascination with her ice cream. Instead of saying anything, he squeezed her hand and went back to eating.

He didn't ask her out.

And he certainly didn't clarify what he'd meant.

She had no idea if she was relieved or disappointed.

As they were loading the girls back into his buggy, Micah noticed a car pull up in front of the Dairy Queen and drop off an older woman who toddled toward the door. Micah hustled over to the door, opened it wide for her and spoke to the woman.

When he jogged back to the buggy and climbed in, Susannah said, "What was that about?"

"An idea."

"What kind of idea?"

"The *gut* kind, of course."

"We want to play I Spy," Sharon said, leaning forward over the seat.

"Best sit back," Susannah said.

"Can we play?"

"I spy with my little eye…" Shiloh was practically bouncing on the seat.

The sugary treat must have given both girls an added burst of energy.

Sharon's voice went up an octave. "I wanna go first."

"But I already spied."

"Did not."

"Did, too. I spied that cat over there." She pointed with her finger to a ginger cat sitting on a picnic table.

"Okay, I know what you spied—a cat. Now it's my turn. I spy…"

Micah figured it was best to play along, so they spent the ride home spying another horse and buggy, a red car, two boys riding bikes and even a woman pushing a child on a swing. It wasn't an easy game to play in the buggy, as the thing the person spied was often left behind. When the girls became frustrated, he changed the game to fifty questions, which went much more smoothly.

By the time they reached Susannah's place, he understood how the girls managed to wear her out. He'd barely pulled the buggy to a stop when both Sharon and Shiloh tumbled out. They clamored up the porch steps, rushing to show their *mamm* the paper place mats they had colored.

"Those two are a handful."

"I told you so."

"They're cute, though."

"You don't mind that I had to bring them along?"

"Why would I mind?"

Susannah shrugged, and he wondered if she was thinking what he was thinking. But if he asked, she'd probably just deny it. Susannah was traditional, and she wouldn't admit to wanting to kiss him or even wanting to be alone with him—not that she'd ever lie, but she wouldn't want to be forward.

As if to confirm his thoughts, she blushed prettily and then glanced away. "I should go fetch the clothes off the line."

"I'll help."

Micah set the brake on the buggy and tethered the horse to the hitching post Thomas has fashioned in front of the house. Then he followed Susannah to the back-yard, thinking about the girls he had dated before, the girls back home. They had been quite different from Susannah. They'd been flirty and immature. He could see that now. They'd covered their insecurities up with bold words and *Englisch* clothes, but they hadn't shared their dreams or fears or hopes for the future.

They'd tried to prove to him they were different, that they were *the one*. The pressure to choose and settle down with one girl had begun when he'd turned twenty-one. His parents didn't understand what he was waiting for. Honestly, he didn't know, either. He'd always felt different from everyone else.

Now he wasn't so sure about that.

Underneath, wasn't everyone the same? Everyone wanted to be liked, to be respected and to have their opinions count.

But it was more than that.

Everyone wanted to connect in some authentic way. Maybe that was what he'd been looking for on social media. He wasn't certain. He only knew that he wasn't finding satisfaction there, but when he was with Susannah, that itch felt as if it was being satisfied. Just watching her fold clothes brought a goofy smile to his face, and he was powerless to stop it. He was confused about his feelings when he was around her, but he was also content for the first time in his life.

How could he feel both things at the same time?

Susannah laughed when she saw the way he was folding the towels.

"Do not tell me I'm doing this wrong."

"Okay."

He looked at the neat stack she'd placed in her basket, then at the towel he'd folded into a football shape. "I'm doing this wrong. Show me."

Instead of pointing out he most certainly did not know the proper way to fold clothes, she walked over to where he was standing.

"Hold the towel up like this."

He picked up a towel and mirrored what she was doing. "Now fold it like this."

He thought he did what she did, but looking down, he must have twisted it somehow.

Susannah started laughing—a sound he dearly loved to hear. "This is impossible," he growled.

"Of course it's not. All you need is practice."

"Uh-huh."

She quickly folded the last of the towels, and they carried the two baskets of fresh laundry to the back porch.

"Are you going to tell me what your *gut* idea was? The one you had when you held the door open for the *Englisch* woman?"

"Hmm...I'd rather wait and see if it pans out."

"So, you're not going to tell me."

"I will say this..." He stepped closer, glanced at the windows to be sure no one was watching and then dipped his head and kissed her softly on the lips. Why did she taste like strawberries? He didn't ask about that. Instead he said, "If it works out, I'll have the money to take you to dinner."

"Will you, now?"

He wanted to kiss her again, but Sharon and Shiloh sprinted out the back door, squealing and running to the swings that had been set up under the branches of a large maple tree.

Susannah stepped toward the porch. "I should probably help with dinner."

"And I need to go and talk to my grandparents about that newspaper thing."

"I suppose it would be best if they hear about it from you before a neighbor takes them a copy."

"And I'll talk to your *dat* tomorrow when I come over."

Which he realized was a change in how he did things. Usually he avoided such conversations. But what was the point in that? Best to stay ahead of trouble if that was even possible, though in this case it might already be too late for that.

Micah knew the minute he stepped into the house that he was indeed too late in beating the bad news home. A copy of the *Goshen News* sat on the kitchen table, where supper should have been. His *daddi* and *mammi* were sitting at the table, obviously waiting for him.

"I was coming home to talk to you about that." He slid into a seat at the table.

When his *daddi* finally looked up, Micah's heart sank. He saw an entire world of emotions in the set of his mouth, the weariness of his eyes and the frown lines that seemed permanently etched on his forehead.

Mammi sat with her hands cradling a cup of coffee. Supper was on the stove, but apparently no one was expecting to eat anytime soon.

His *daddi* sighed heavily, as if he were carrying the weight of the world and needed to set it down. "We're disappointed, Micah."

"But I can explain."

"How can you explain that?" His voice remained a low growl.

Micah could have handled a raised voice. Hadn't he just told Susannah about how his parents would holler at each other? But always, always they would make up before darkness fell on the day. No, what his *daddi*'s voice told him was that he'd already made up his mind, already decided on his judgment and there would be no arguing.

Still, he had to try.

"I did take the picture."

"With the *Englisch* phone."

"I had never been to a barn raising with so many people, and I wanted to show my *schweschdern*."

"We make quite an effort to keep the *Englisch* photographers at bay, only to have you splash our doings on the front page of the local paper." *Daddi* grabbed the paper from the table and shook it at Micah. "I don't know what you were thinking, but I do know that I warned you."

"But I didn't—"

"We are to remain separate, Micah. Do you not understand what that means?"

"I did *not* send that picture in to the paper."

"Now you're denying taking it?"

"*Nein.* I took it, but someone else sent it in."

"That makes no sense."

"It was a friend of mine."

"An *Englisch* friend, no doubt."

"He thought he was helping me. He thought I could use the money, but he didn't ask me first. I had no idea he would do such a thing."

"You should have considered that possibility before you took the photograph." *Daddi* dropped the paper and slapped the flat of his palm against the table. "If you hadn't taken it to begin with, we wouldn't be having this discussion."

"What is so wrong with people seeing that we help one another?" Micah knew his temper was winning out over his common sense, but he couldn't help it. He couldn't sit there and not defend himself.

"Go and get the phone."

"What?"

"You heard me. Go and get the phone."

Micah didn't have to go and get the phone, since it was still in his pocket from having gone to town. He handed it to his *daddi*, thinking that perhaps he was going to keep it awhile or hand it over to the bishop or mail it back home to his parents. He never once thought that the man would drop it on the floor, stand and crush it beneath his foot.

"Are you crazy? Do you know how much that cost?"

"Perhaps you should learn to use your money more wisely, then." He didn't bother to pick up the pieces. Instead he snatched his hat off the hook on the wall. "I'm warning you again, Micah. You step outside the lines one more time—"

"And are those lines that you've drawn? Or the bishop? Because last time I spoke with Thomas, he was quite happy with my work."

"Your work—yes. But your actions outside work? You should stop and consider the repercussions of those, Micah. As far as I'm concerned, you're on your last chance." *Daddi* didn't even turn to look at him. Something about the stoop of the man's shoulders pulled guilt strings in Micah's heart, and if he'd even turned and given him a hint of compassion he might have let his sympathy for his grandfather win over his anger.

But he didn't turn.

He didn't look at him.

And Micah quickly brushed away any such thoughts of sympathy. His *daddi* was obstinate and unfair. He did not deserve anyone's sympathy.

"Go against our *Ordnung* one more time, and you'll have to find another place to live."

"You're kicking me out?"

Now *Daddi* did turn. The stump of his right arm rested in the pocket that *Mammi* had sewn from the sleeve. His left hand was tanned and strong. At the moment he was using it to rub a circle on his chest.

"Maybe you should calm down, John." It was the first words his *mammi* had spoken.

"I'm fine." He never took his eyes off Micah. "The

crops are in. I won't need your help around here except for feeding the horses and cleaning out the stalls."

"Meaning what?"

"Meaning I want you to find another job." And with that final jab, he turned and left the house.

Micah sat staring at the door his *daddi* had walked through.

Why did life have to be like this?

Why did his grandfather make a problem where there was none?

Mammi stood, fetched the broom and dustpan and swept up the pieces of phone. She held the dustpan out to him. "Want what's left of it?"

He waved her away.

"Your *daddi*…"

"I know. He wants what's best for me."

"It's true, Micah. Whether you can see it or not, it's true."

"Is it also true that he doesn't need me around here to help him? Or does he just not *want* me around to help him? Because it's pretty plain to me that he can't stand the sight of me."

"You're being unfair."

"*He*'s being unfair."

His *mammi* had never been particularly demonstrative with her emotions, but now she sat down beside him and pulled his hands into her lap. "He's a *gut* man, your *daddi*, and I won't have you disrespecting him."

Her words were softened by her touch as she reached out and untwisted one of his suspenders. "John's not a proud man, but he sees things as black-and-white. He wants you to put away your childhood things…"

"By stomping on them?"

"Become a man and put away childish things."

"And get another job."

"Only for the mornings. You'll continue to help Thomas in the afternoons." She patted him on the shoulder, stood and walked to the stove. "Dinner will be ready in thirty minutes."

Micah wanted to say he wasn't hungry, but in truth his stomach was gurgling. Refusing to eat would be childish, plus he would go to bed hungry. There was no use trying to avoid his *daddi*, and he wasn't ready to move out. The thought hadn't really ever occurred to him.

He'd thought of moving home, but not of moving out.

Where would he go?

And how would he afford it?

Nein. He needed to find a way to make this work until he could return to Maine, which meant he needed a job. He remembered the older *Englisch* woman, the car that had dropped her off, the sign in the window of the car.

The idea he'd had would put extra money in his pocket and satisfy his *daddi*'s demands. As to whether they would approve of what he hoped to do, time would tell.

Chapter Eight

Susannah did not plan on telling her *mamm* about the kiss.

But as they were sitting at the kitchen table later that evening—her *mamm* knitting and Susannah stitching together the top of a nine-patch quilt—the details of the day came tumbling out of her mouth.

If her *mamm* was surprised, she hid it well.

"You've been kissed before."

"*Ya*, but it's been a while."

"Since before your cancer."

"Just about two years ago, which doesn't say much for my dating life."

"You know, Susannah, you're not damaged goods."

"Why would you say that?" Susannah pricked her finger with the needle, jerked her hand away and inspected it to make sure she wouldn't bleed on the fabric.

"I sometimes think that you have the opinion that no one would want you, that you're not whole."

"I'm not whole. The doctors removed part of me, leaving me not whole."

"Not true." Her *mamm* shook her head so vigorously

that her *kapp* strings bounced. It reminded Susannah so much of Sharon that she couldn't help smiling. "You are fearfully and wonderfully made."

"Is now really the time to quote Scripture?"

"If it fits, then yes, it is."

Susannah ducked her head to better see the seam she was attempting to stitch. In truth, her mother's words brought tears to her eyes. Some days she hated that she cried so easily, that she was so emotional. Other days it seemed as if she was viewing life from a distance and couldn't feel a thing. She wasn't sure which was worse.

"After my diagnosis, Samuel treated me differently, almost as if I was contagious."

"It's obvious now to both of us that you and Samuel were not meant to be anything more than *freinden*."

"I wish it had been obvious then. At the time, the way he treated me and then our breakup… It just—well it hurt."

"And if I could have spared you that hurt I would have."

"It doesn't bother me much anymore, not really. I've moved on." As she uttered those words, words she'd probably said before, Susannah was surprised to find that they were true in a new way. Thinking of Samuel didn't bring the old ache that it had at one time.

"My point is that your cancer wasn't something that *Gotte* didn't see coming. It wasn't a mistake on His part."

"How could it have been intentional?"

"I don't know. Most of the whys in life I don't understand."

"What you're saying doesn't make any sense."

"Do you think that Caroline Byers's *bruder* is a mistake?"

"Because he has Down syndrome? Of course not."

"He's not damaged goods?"

"You know that no one thinks that." She glanced up to see her *mamm* studying her very closely. "A person who is born different isn't damaged in the way that a buggy might be after a wreck."

"I'm glad you feel that way."

"We all do. We all love Stephen. Have you seen how he is with their sheep? He's named every one, and they come to him when he calls them. Stephen isn't damaged. He's special."

"So *Gotte* didn't make a mistake with him?"

"I don't know why he's different, but the fact that he is doesn't cause anyone to love him any less. So no, I don't think *Gotte* made a mistake."

"You'd never throw him away."

Now her *mamm* was teasing her. Sure enough, when Susannah glanced up, she noticed a smile tugging at her *mamm*'s lips.

"I would not, and no one who knows him would."

"Then how are you any different?"

"I don't follow."

"Only because you're being stubborn."

Instead of asking her *mamm* to explain, Susannah allowed a silence to permeate the room. She became aware of the sound of her mother's knitting needles, the crickets outside, the creak of her father's rocking chair from where he sat on the porch.

Finally, Susannah gave up on the seam that was growing increasingly crooked. She stood, heated water on the stove and brought two cups of tea and a plate of oatmeal bars to the table.

"Danki."

"Gem gschehne."

And those words, that tradition of gratefulness and kindness, seemed to loosen the cat's grip on Susannah's tongue.

"I don't think I'm damaged, but I do think I'm different."

"Every one of *Gotte*'s creatures is unique."

"And maybe it wasn't a mistake that I had cancer. Maybe *Gotte* has some grand plan, some greater good that will come from it."

"He used Balaam's donkey. I'm sure He can use your cancer."

"But I am different, *Mamm*. There's no more use in denying that than there would be in denying that Stephen is different."

Her *mamm* nodded and reached for an oatmeal bar.

"So what are you really worried about?"

Susannah sipped her tea, then sighed and closed her eyes for a moment. When she opened them, her *mamm* was studying her.

"That the kiss meant nothing to Micah and everything to me. That the kiss meant everything to both of us. That he doesn't understand the baggage that I carry around with me—that there is a chance the cancer will return."

"And there's an even better chance that it won't."

"Regardless, I will not be able to have children."

Her *mamm* didn't answer right away. In fact, Susannah thought she wouldn't. They finished their snack, her *mamm* stood, rinsed their cups, covered the oatmeal bars with a dish towel and finally sat down across from her again.

"If Micah loves you—and I'm not suggesting that's true or that enduring love always follows one kiss—but if he does, then it won't matter to him whether or not you can have children."

"How can it *not* matter to him?" As hard as she tried to blink away the tears, they insisted on coursing down her cheeks. Her *mamm* reached forward and thumbed them away, then kissed her on the forehead.

"Because love doesn't work that way."

Micah spoke with Thomas early the next morning. As he laid out the details of his plan, he noticed Thomas's hesitancy and expression of skepticism.

"I'd like your approval to just try this—give it a few weeks, a month at the most. If it doesn't work, then I'll try to find employment at one of the businesses in town."

"And you've spoken to your *daddi* about this?"

"*Nein.* I wanted your approval first, and I also still need to speak with Widow Miller and finalize the details. Once everything is in place, I'll go to *Daddi* and explain the entire thing. You have my word on that."

Thomas clasped him on the back. "And you've prayed about this?"

"I have, and I feel that *Gotte* put this idea in my mind. I certainly would have never thought of it on my own."

"All from seeing a driver drop a woman off at the Dairy Queen." They were sitting in the farrier shop. Thomas had been working on his accounting books. He picked up a pen, clicked it twice and sat it back down. "Coincidence or possibly *Gotte*'s guiding hand."

"I honestly think it's something I'd be *gut* at. I have a lot of energy, it drives me crazy to sit still and I have an outgoing personality."

"That you do." Thomas glanced around his farrier

shop. "I can take care of today's work. See if you can get the details of your plan worked out."

"*Danki.*"

Micah was almost to the door when Thomas called him back. "Perhaps it would help if we switched your hours with me to the morning. That way you could work on your new business into the early evening when necessary."

"You'd be willing to do that?"

"Sure. Seems to me you'd have a more flexible schedule then, to accommodate your customers."

"What about our meetings, you know, where I'm learning to be properly Amish?"

"I suppose we can talk while we're working, like we are now."

Micah wanted to jump and shout at the same time. Instead, he smiled his thanks and headed down the lane. Widow Miller lived two miles away. He'd be walking that distance twice a day, but Micah didn't mind. He could cover a mile in twenty minutes, and the exercise would do him good.

He'd met the older woman when he and Thomas had gone to her house to shoe her buggy horse. The gelding was not getting enough exercise and generally wasn't being looked after as well as he should have been. Nothing neglectful, really, but the horse could use a good brushing and the buggy definitely needed to be cleaned.

It took him ten minutes to explain his plan and another twenty to work out the details. Thirty minutes later, he was ready to go to the Goshen Library to make some flyers and copy them, but first he needed his *daddi*'s approval.

* * *

"Just once, why can't you do something normal?"

Micah had dared to hope that his *daddi* would be as open-minded as Thomas. Apparently that was hoping for too much. He tried to tap down his anger—count to five, take deep breaths, be patient. It wasn't working. He could feel his pulse accelerating and sweat running down his back.

How he would love to storm out of the barn, but that was what a child would do. He was a man now, and he was ready to act like one. He was ready to stand and fight for what he wanted to do.

"You want me to go and work at the RV factory? Or maybe you see me riding over to Amish Acres every day, showing *Englischers* what it's like to live simply."

"There's nothing wrong with either one of those jobs."

Micah took a deep breath. "I didn't say there was, but I think my idea is something I could be successful at."

"And Thomas approved of it?"

"He did. He even offered to shift my hours to mornings."

His *daddi* turned back to the plow blade that he was sharpening. He'd positioned the blade in a bench vise to hold it steady. It was amazing what the man had learned to do with one arm.

"And you'll be splitting what you earn with Widow Miller?"

"Fifty-fifty. Seems only fair since I'll be using her buggy and horse. Plus, it'll be better for the horse."

"So you explained."

Micah waited, and it seemed that his *daddi* had forgotten he was there. Finally, he raised his good arm and made a motion as if he was shooing away a fly. "I expect you to make good on what you told Thomas. If you're not seeing enough business in two weeks…"

"We agreed to a month."

"And if the widow is unhappy with the deal for any reason, then you abandon this plan and get a real job."

"Done."

If he'd been expecting his *daddi*'s blessing, he might have stood there a long time. Instead, he took his grandfather's grunt as permission, hitched their mare to the buggy and headed to town to make it to the library before it closed.

Susannah and her *mamm* had planned to go to a sew-in the following Monday. She hadn't seen Micah on Sunday, but then perhaps his grandparents had lunch with someone else. It was their off Sunday. She was a little surprised that he hadn't stopped by, but then it wasn't like he'd promised he would.

The sew-in would be a nice distraction. Sharon and Shiloh were excited to see their friends, but if Susannah was honest with herself, she was rather dreading the entire thing. There was no doubt that she'd be grilled about Micah's comings and goings. He seemed to be the talk of the town these days, which just proved that very little was happening in May in Goshen, Indiana.

But her mother was looking forward to her day off the farm, and Susannah knew that begging off would make things harder since she wouldn't be there to help keep an eye on the twins. It would actually be selfish for her to do so when there was no good reason not to go, and besides she'd just have to face everyone at the next Sunday meeting. Might as well get it over with on a beautiful summer day.

The sew-in had been scheduled so they could complete half a dozen quilts that they planned to donate to the school auction held every summer. That event attracted *Englischers* with money to spend on authentic Amish items. The funds raised helped to pay for school supplies as well as any needed repairs to the building.

She found herself growing more excited as her *mamm* drove the buggy toward Widow Miller's, where the sew-in was to take place.

After they'd parked the buggy, Susannah asked Sharon and Shiloh to help her. "Can each of you carry in one of our lunch dishes?"

"I can carry the big one." Shiloh stood up straight and tall as if to prove her strength.

"Better give me the little one," Sharon said. "I drop sometimes."

"Both of you hold the dish with both hands and walk—don't run."

Taking their task very seriously, they walked toward Widow Miller's front porch and up the steps.

"They're *gut* girls." Her *mamm* hooked her arm through Susannah's. "You've been rather quiet today."

"Have I?"

"Anything you want to talk about?"

"I'm dreading everyone asking me questions about Micah."

"And why would you dread that?"

"First of all, because I'm not his keeper."

"But you are his friend, and it's normal for people to be curious."

"I suppose. And second, folks seem to assume the worst where Micah is concerned. I guess his first impression wasn't a particularly *gut* one."

"You can set the record straight."

And then they were in the widow's house, and the large group of women assembled there naturally separated into smaller groups by generational lines. Susannah supposed that was because friendships had formed many years ago, and there weren't that many chances to all get together and catch up. Sometimes it seemed to Susannah that she knew more about her cousins in Ohio than she did about someone living down the street.

She went out the back door. Two quilts had been set up on standing looms. Around one was most of the sixteen-to-eighteen-year-old group. She remembered how she'd looked forward to these days when she was first out of school. She hadn't missed sitting in a school desk for the majority of the day, but she'd certainly missed seeing her friends. Watching that younger group brought a sharp pain of nostalgia that she hadn't expected.

Did she miss being so young?

It wasn't as if she was an old maid now.

But then she turned toward her group, which was gathered around a double-wedding-ring quilt that had also been placed on a quilt stand. They were situated more toward the side yard, with a view of both the back and the front of the house. It seemed to her that over half the group was pregnant. Many of the others had babies in carriers on the ground beside them. Only Susannah, Deborah and three other girls remained unmarried.

Perhaps she didn't really fit in with either group, which was a rather depressing thought. Regardless, there was quilting to be done.

She clenched her teeth and prayed for patience.

Strangely, no one asked her a thing about Micah. There was plenty of "How are you today, Susannah?"

and "What a pretty apron. Is that new?" and "I saw your *schweschdern* flitting around here. They certainly are growing."

She felt herself relax, so much so that when she saw looks passing between others—knowing looks—she convinced herself that it had nothing to do with her or Micah.

They'd sewn for most of the morning when she heard the clatter of buggy wheels.

Again the knowing looks, and then as one, they stopped sewing and turned their attention toward the front of the house.

And that was when she saw him. Micah was driving Widow Miller's buggy. When he pulled to a stop, he jumped out, walked around the buggy and helped out Old Sally. It was when he closed the buggy door after her that Susannah saw the sign.

It read Amish Taxi, followed by a phone number.

Micah had helped Old Sally up the porch steps. As he returned to his buggy, he stopped and waved—whether at Susannah or the group in general, she wasn't sure.

He looked inordinately pleased with himself.

And Susannah suddenly wished she could melt into the ground because conversations had erupted to her right and her left, and they were all about Micah and his new business.

She didn't have a moment alone with Deborah until they were eating lunch.

As usual, Sharon and Shiloh had finished in record time, so Susannah took her plate of food out to the picnic table that was situated next to the swings and seesaw, long ago remnants of a time when Naomi Miller had *kinner* and *grandkinner* around. Now all of her family lived in Shipshewana—close enough to visit, but not as often as she'd like. Susannah wondered why she hadn't moved with her family. Before she could think that through, they were surrounded by loud, energetic children. The afternoon was filled with a dozen girls and boys running and shouting and using up their abundance of energy.

Deborah nudged her with her shoulder. "You really didn't know?"

"I really didn't."

"It was the only topic of conversation before you got here, and then I tried to get your attention."

"You did?"

"*Ya.* I was…" Deborah pantomimed raising her hand above her head and bringing it back down over her *kapp*.

"Thought you were swatting at a bee."

"Word is he started this morning, but he put out flyers all over the community on Saturday."

"Good grief, word travels fast."

"You know the Amish grapevine."

Susannah momentarily covered her face with her hands.

"It's not so bad."

"Not so bad? Amish Taxi? It sounds like a bad joke."

"But it is honest labor, and to hear the girls talk, he had your father's approval."

"What?" Susannah's voice rose so high that both Sharon and Shiloh turned to look at her. She waved at them to go back to playing. "My *dat* knew and didn't tell me?"

"You've told me before that he's very private about things that he discusses with others."

"That's true."

"Seems to me it's honest work, and what else is he to do? The crops are in and…"

"And there are at least a dozen people hiring in Goshen to help with summer tourists."

"I suspect he'll have a line of folks waiting to ride in an Amish Taxi. He'll be helping with tourists plenty." Deborah started laughing and then, against her better instincts, Susannah joined her. It was rather funny if you thought about it.

It wasn't until they were all back home and had finished eating dinner that she had a chance to talk to her *dat* about it. Sharon and Shiloh were upstairs preparing for bed. Playing with the other children all day had certainly worn them out. They'd practically fallen asleep with their *kapp* strings in their soup.

"Seemed like a rather *gut* idea to me," Thomas said. "He's splitting what he earns with the widow, since he's using her buggy and horse."

"He is?"

"The horse needs more exercise, and Widow Miller can certainly use the money."

"She needs money?"

"It's not easy for the older ones." Her *mamm* filled their mugs with decaffeinated coffee.

"What do you mean?" Susannah asked.

"About what?"

"About it not being easy on the older folks. I thought we… Well, I thought that we provided for those in our community who had less."

"We do, as is right and proper." Her *dat* pointed an unlit pipe at her. He'd had it for as long as she could remember. She'd asked her *mamm* about it once. The pipe had been his father's. He only actually smoked it once a day, only after the evening meal, and only out on the porch. "The Scripture tells us as much—to care for the orphans and the widows."

"Many of our elders have family close by, but for those who don't, finances can be tight. They'll never want for house repairs or groceries, but even Widow Miller likes to have a little extra change in her pocketbook."

"She has family in Shipshe."

"That she does, but there's some difficulty there. She doesn't ask them for extra because she doesn't think they have it."

Susannah shook her head. "We're getting off topic here. How is Micah's business even supposed to work?"

"Maybe you should ask him yourself." Her *dat* pointed the pipe toward the window, where she could just make out Micah crossing the field that separated her parents' home from his grandparents.

Susannah ignored the smile that passed between her parents, excused herself and met Micah before he'd made it to the porch.

"Amish Taxi? Really?"

"I'm sorry I didn't get a chance to tell you myself."

"You certainly don't owe me an explanation." The words came out snippier than she intended, so she looked up, down and around, and then asked, "Wanna look at Shiloh's kittens?"

Instead of answering, he entwined his fingers with hers, and that seemed so right, felt so natural, that she couldn't possibly hold on to her frustration. Fifteen minutes later they'd examined each kitten. There were five in all—four striped and one white.

"We never had any cats growing up." Micah ran his finger from the top of the white kitten's head, along its spine, to the tail. He was rewarded with a purr that resembled a small power motor. He glanced up at her and smiled. "This one likes me."

"You never had barn cats?"

"*Nein*. My *mamm* was allergic. If we had church in a member's barn and they had cats, she'd start sneezing and her eyes would water, and she'd have to excuse herself and go outside."

"You don't seem allergic."

"Guess not." He placed the kitten down next to the mama cat. They walked outside and stood looking at the near-dark sky.

Susannah could make out the first star, but there was still enough light for her to turn and study Micah. "Tell me how this new business of yours is supposed to work."

"Pretty simple, really. Widow Miller lets me know ahead of time if she will need the horse and buggy. Mostly she only drives to church or the grocery store or sometimes a doctor's appointment. It was one of the things that made me think of it. Her horse—Sunny Boy—needs more exercise. He almost seemed depressed when your *dat* and I went over to shoe him last time."

"Okay. So you walk to her house, harness Sunny Boy to the buggy and then…"

"I bought another phone, but not like the last one. This one doesn't even have the internet. It's only for making and receiving calls." He had to explain to her about his *daddi* crushing his cell phone and insisting he get a job.

"I'm sorry, Micah. I had no idea he was so strict."

Micah shrugged. "I don't think it's about me as much as it is about him coming to terms with the changes around him."

"That's awfully mature of you to say."

"I've never been accused of being mature before." He

stepped out from under the overhang of the barn. "Want to walk a little? For some reason, I'm feeling restless."

So they walked, and they talked some more as the moon rose and darkness fell properly over the fields.

He'd had a dozen rides his first day of business.

He'd made two hundred dollars.

Half of that he gave to the widow when he returned the horse and buggy.

Susannah thought of what her *dat* had said about helping the elderly. Micah was certainly doing that.

"This morning I worked a couple of hours for your *dat*, and when things slowed down, he told me to go on to town and get started on my new venture."

"I can see why my *dat* gave you his approval, but I'm a little surprised your *daddi* went along with it."

"Guess he felt like he didn't have a choice, since the bishop had approved."

"But he wasn't happy."

"Nein."

"Maybe he will be, when he sees how you're helping folks."

"Half of my customers were *Englisch*, just wanting to ride in an authentic buggy."

"That's pretty common around here."

"Not so much in Maine." Micah's voice turned somber. "*Daddi* thinks we should be separate. I'm sure that's the part of my plan that he doesn't approve of…as if being around *Englischers* will rub off on me. Next thing you know, I'll be wearing blue jeans and carrying a cell phone."

"You were wearing blue jeans the first day I saw you."

"True."

"And you had a phone in your back pocket."

"See? I'm already corrupted, so what harm can come?"

What harm indeed. Susannah had heard every possible scenario as she'd sat in the sewing circle. Everything from he shouldn't be alone with *Englisch* girls to he might put Timothy Zook out of business. Timothy ran a buggy ride for *Englischers* during the summer, and Susannah knew for a fact that he had more business than he cared to have. He had refused to extend his hours and had even cut his days back to three a week. Micah would actually be filling a gap that needed to be filled, and he'd be helping Amish folks at the same time.

She understood in that moment that Micah was a good person. It was only that he considered things from a different perspective than most. Who else would have thought of being an Amish taxi driver?

She walked over to an old tree that held a tire swing.

"Get in," he said.

"What is it with you and swings?"

"Just get in already. I'll push."

"I'm not even sure it will hold me."

Micah tugged on the rope, looked up at the limb and declared it sound.

He turned the tire upside down and ran his hand inside to make sure there was no water or critters, then he held it high as she wiggled her shoulders through. And the next thing Susannah knew, the tire swing was going up, then down and twirling and then back up again, and all of the responsibilities that she carried on her shoulders—or thought she did—fell away. Suddenly she was simply a young woman in a swing being pushed by a handsome young man. And above her the stars seemed to wink their approval.

Chapter Nine

What Micah didn't share with Susannah was that he was giving his grandparents half of his portion of the day's earnings. Out of two hundred dollars, the widow received one hundred, his grandparents fifty, and he kept fifty. It seemed like a fair enough arrangement to him. His grandparents were providing him a place to stay and feeding him. He also received a small amount each week for working with Thomas Beiler in the farrier shop. Between the two jobs, he felt like he was pulling his weight.

He would be lying to himself if he didn't admit that he thought his grandfather would thank him, or at least acknowledge in some way that he'd done well.

Instead, the next morning his grandfather had ignored the money sitting on the middle of the table. When his *mammi* brought it up, he'd simply grunted and told her to put it in the mason jar she kept in the pantry. "Something's bound to break soon, and we'll need it."

The meal passed in silence, the way most of their meals did, and then without another word, his *daddi* stood, pushed in his chair and walked out toward the barn.

"Has he always been like this?" Micah asked.

"Like what?" His *mammi* stood and began clearing away the breakfast dishes.

"Solemn, taciturn, grumpy."

Mammi had her back to him as she filled the kitchen sink with warm water and then a splash of dish-washing detergent, but he could still make out the heavy sigh.

He carried the rest of the dishes to her and picked up a dish towel. "I'll dry if you wash."

Which seemed to ease her burden a bit.

Was it that easy?

Did helping with dishes make that big a difference?

Or was it more that his grandmother wanted to be seen, that she wanted to be thanked for her labors the same way that Micah wanted to be thanked for the fifty dollars sitting on the table? When was the last time someone had thanked her for making a meal or putting clean sheets on the bed or sweeping the floors?

"Breakfast was *gut*."

"*Ya?*"

"*Mamm* never did learn how to make biscuits from scratch."

Mammi started laughing. "I tried teaching her, and I know her mother tried, as well. She always seemed to forget at least one ingredient, and there aren't that many ingredients in biscuits."

"I might have starved if Becky hadn't taken over the cooking."

"Your *schweschdern* are all *gut* girls. It's funny when you think about it. I suppose we all have things that we're good at and other things that we never can quite get the hang of."

They continued washing and drying, and Micah was surprised to find that the silence between them felt comfortable. He realized he'd miss this when he went home—this time with grandparents that he barely knew.

"I wish I could figure out how to talk to him. Everything I say seems to irritate him one way or another."

"Your *daddi* never was much of a conversationalist."

"So it's not just me?"

"*Nein*, though…" She shook her head, as if she wished she hadn't started the sentence that she couldn't bring herself to finish.

"Might as well say it."

"It's only that he worries about you. Your *dat* was our only son, and now you're his only son."

"I'm supposed to carry on the family name."

"I don't know about that. If the Lord wills it…"

"But…"

"But you do have a responsibility to your family, even to your *schweschdern*."

Micah was shaking his head before she'd even finished. "They're all older than me. Trust me—they're not depending on me for anything."

"That's not true." *Mammi* pulled the plug on the sink water and watched it swirl down the drain. "It might seem that way now, because of your age. And you'll always hold a special place in their hearts because you're the baby *bruder* they hoped and prayed for. But when you're older—when you're forty or fifty or sixty—it won't matter that you're the youngest. They'll look to you for advice. It's just the way Amish families are."

"Hard to imagine."

"I know it is."

The sun was peeking over the horizon, and he had chores to do before heading over to work at the bishop's. Hopefully, his afternoon would once again be full of taxi customers. He was looking forward to the day, and he felt some better about his grandfather. He might never understand him, but at least he could sympathize a little with what the old guy was going through.

He'd given his grandmother a quick hug, fetched his hat and was headed out the back door when his *mammi* called him back. "Keep an eye on him for me."

"Daddi?"

"Ya, just…let me know if you notice he's not feeling well."

"Is he not feeling well?"

"Nothing that he would admit to." She walked over to him, straightened his hat and stood on tiptoes to kiss his cheek. "But as you so clearly pointed out, he's grumpier than ever. It could be that he's feeling worse than he's letting on."

As he walked to the barn, Micah realized that it wasn't *Daddi*'s amputated arm that *Mammi* was talking about. *Daddi* had been dealing with that longer than Micah had been alive. No, if he wasn't feeling well, it was something else, and it was something that he wasn't even talking to *Mammi* about. The question was whether it was anything serious, and if it was, how they'd convince him to see a doctor about it.

The next day, Susannah stood and stared at the calendar on the wall. She'd had the day circled since her last visit, six months before.

"Are you sure you don't want me to go with you?" Her *mamm* was sewing new dresses for Shiloh and Sharon on the old treadle machine they kept in Susannah's shop. Susannah had offered to do it, but in truth, she was better with quilts than she was with garments.

"*Nein.* I can go by myself."

"We'll go with you, Susannah." Sharon was sitting on the floor playing with a ball and jacks.

"We can hold your hand," Shiloh said from her chair beside the sewing machine, where she was watching her mother sew each stitch.

"By the time you get home, these two girls will have nice new frocks."

"Because we're growing," Shiloh said.

"Like weeds. That's what *Dat* said. 'You girls are growing like weeds.'" Sharon's imitation of their *dat* caused everyone to laugh and eased the worry that Susannah was feeling.

As she directed their buggy horse, Percy, toward town, she realized she wasn't terribly worried about what the doctor would say. There was always a chance that her cancer would return, but wouldn't she know it? Wouldn't she feel different?

The fear of what might happen was something she'd learned to live with—at least some days. Other days were a bit harder. All she knew for certain was that she felt better, healthier than she had in a very long time. Her cancer no longer was something that she thought about constantly. It no longer defined her, or at least she didn't think it did. She was enjoying being a normal young woman, and she wasn't ready for that to change. Not yet. Maybe not ever.

She'd stopped by for blood work the week before.

Today she would have an examination and then meet with the doctor to discuss her test results.

Dr. Kelly's office always made Susannah smile—it was decorated with pictures from her patients, some who were obviously quite young. The drawings sported stick figures holding a stethoscope, large hearts decorating each person and flowers taller than the people.

As the doctor walked in and picked up a folder, Susannah was overwhelmed by a fluttery feeling in her stomach—it wasn't fear exactly, but some emotion just as powerful.

"Your test results look good."

"They do?" The butterflies in her stomach scattered, replaced by sudden and total euphoria.

"Were you expecting something else?" Dr. Kelly had black skin, shoulder-length hair and kind eyes. She seemed ageless, but the picture of two teenage boys on her desk—boys Susannah could tell by one glance were her sons—indicated she had to be close to forty. "Talk to me, Susannah. Having you been feeling poorly?"

"Nein. I feel fine, and I wasn't expecting anything else. I always hope and pray the tests will come back fine, but I also try to prepare myself. You know…"

"Go on."

"Well, I try to weigh myself a couple of times a week to make sure I'm not losing weight, because last time…"

"I remember how thin you'd become when you first came to me."

"And I keep the journal you had me start…saying how I feel each day."

"That's good, Susannah. It's good that you're being vigilant about your health and keeping your appointments. Everything here looks fine. In fact, you seem healthier— and happier—than I've seen you in a long time."

Dr. Kelly waited. She didn't check her watch or tap her fingers against the desktop. If anything, she relaxed into her chair, indicating Susannah could take her time sorting through her emotions.

"Can I ask you a question?"

"Of course."

"How many of your patients, patients my age, go on to live happy lives—happily married lives?"

"That's an interesting question. I'd say roughly about the same percentage as those without cancer."

"Oh."

"I just read a study that Americans are waiting longer to marry, and more people than ever before are choosing not to marry at all. But that's probably not true among the Amish."

"It's not true among the Amish I know. Most Amish pair up by the time they're twenty, and they stay married for life."

Dr. Kelly sat there, her fingertips steepled together, for another moment. Then she crossed her arms on the desk and leaned forward. "I can tell you my opinion, but it's based on purely anecdotal evidence."

Susannah nodded, though she wasn't completely sure what anecdotal evidence was.

"It seems that my patients put their lives on hold when they first receive their cancer diagnoses. If they're young and just beginning to consider marrying, they put that out of their mind for a while. If they're older and were thinking of retiring and traveling the US, they put that on hold. They press the pause button on their lives and deal with their cancer."

"And then?"

"And then the vast majority of them move on. They press the go button. They take up where they left off. Not all of them, of course. For some people, a cancer diagnosis becomes a new identity and changes the way they view every facet of their lives. They don't know how to move past it." She stood, smiled and walked around the desk, before sitting in a chair across from Susannah.

"I have a feeling that what you're experiencing, the thing that's worrying you, is that you are ready to press that go button. And if you're looking for my permission or approval to do so, then you have it. You've always had it. Now all you need is to find the courage to do so."

Susannah didn't remember driving home.

Once there, Shiloh and Shannon pounced on her, insisting she sit in the living room until they ran upstairs and tried on their new dresses. Her *mamm* knew she had good news before she said a word, and when her *dat* came in for dinner, he immediately enfolded her in a hug.

"*Gotte* is *gut*," he murmured, and Susannah nodded her head in agreement.

The rest of the evening passed in a blur. It was when she was kneeling by her bed to say her prayers, which sometimes felt childish but mostly felt necessary, that she realized she was ready to push that go button Dr. Kelly had talked about. She understood in that moment that she was tired of worrying about what might or might not happen.

Would her feelings for Micah grow even stronger?

Did he feel the same?

What would they do when he moved back to Maine?

What if her cancer returned?

And beyond all those questions, there were several that had been in her mind since she'd first learned she had cancer. Would someone really want to marry her knowing that she couldn't have children? Would it be selfish of her to do such a thing? How would she know if any marriage proposal was motivated by true love or something done out of pity?

As she knelt there on the hardwood floor, she didn't receive any answers straight from heaven, but she did resolve to stop worrying and trust that God had a plan.

Micah's afternoons driving Amish and *Englischers* grew even busier than that first day. The following week, Old Eli actually flagged him down from the side of the road. "Heard you're giving rides, and my wife says I can't drive anymore on account of my cataracts."

"I'm headed back to town now. Want a lift?"

"That's why I'm standing out here flagging you down."

Micah generally didn't quote a price for his rides. People paid what they could—most offered something between five and ten dollars. It added up quickly. When he didn't have any Amish folks who needed a lift, he drove to downtown Goshen, parked near the Old Bag Factory and put his cardboard sign out.

Amish Taxi.

$10/person for twenty minutes.

Inevitably, there was a queue of people by the time he returned with the first passenger.

The day flew by. He lost track of how much he'd made, but he thought he'd exceeded the previous day's total. It seemed word was spreading quickly, and he already had rides lined up for each day the next week. After he'd dropped off the last *Englischer* for the day—a lady who simply wanted to drive through the countryside and look at the farms—he stopped by the general store.

"Can I help you?" One of the Amish girls from their church district was working the register. She looked to be about sixteen years old and had freckles across her cheeks and nose. Micah might have been introduced to her at church, but he couldn't remember her name.

"I guess I need a calendar."

"Like a wall calendar?"

"*Nein.* Something I can put in my pocket."

"I know just what you're talking about."

Unfortunately, they all looked pretty girlie to him—the outsides decorated with flowers and hearts and motivational slogans. He settled for the one with kittens, since it reminded him of the white cat he'd held at Susannah's. He bought a pen as well, and at the last minute he spied a display of rose-scented goat lotion. "This stuff work?"

"I guess. My *mammi* uses it."

So he added a tube to his purchases. When was the last time someone had bought his *mammi* a gift? Probably not in the last ten years, since it seemed his *daddi* had been in a bad mood at least that long. He carried his purchases to the register.

"The calendar must be for your Amish taxi business."

"It is."

"I think what you're doing is so smart. Some people say it's a travesty—that's the word Ruth Lapp used when she was in here earlier—but I'm not sure what that means."

"It's bad."

"I gathered as much. Still and all, if you're going to be Amish in this day and age, you have to learn to adapt."

"Not something we're well-known for."

"I'm aware."

"I'm Micah, by the way."

"I'm Lydia." She smiled at him, her cheeks a rosy red.

Did she think he was flirting with her? The old Micah would have been. Maybe out of habit he'd done or said something that she'd taken the wrong way.

"Can you ring me up one more of those tubes of lotion?"

"Sure."

"It's for my girlfriend, Susannah Beiler. Maybe you know her?"

"*Ya*, I know Susannah. I didn't know you two were stepping out." She fetched another tube of the lotion, and then placed all of his items in a bag and counted out his change. "If it doesn't work out with Susannah, you know where to find me."

It was a rather bold statement coming from an Amish girl, but somehow the way she said it, the words seemed more friendly than flirty.

Instead of responding, he waved goodbye and moseyed out to the buggy. The week had turned into a fine one even if it had suffered a rocky start. Maybe by the time he got home, his *daddi* would have found something to smile about, or maybe he needed to stop worrying about whether that would happen. He hadn't caused the old guy's unhappiness; at least he hadn't caused all of it, so there was little chance he could help him get over it.

He returned the buggy and horse to Widow Miller, counted out her portion of the money and turned down oatmeal cookies and milk.

"*Mammi* serves dinner pretty early. Wouldn't want to ruin my appetite."

But as he drew close to his grandfather's place, he saw a van parked in the lane, and he knew that he wouldn't be eating anytime soon.

He rushed up the front porch steps, where his *mammi* stood on one side of the screen door and a reporter for the *Goshen News* stood on the other.

"Micah, I've told this woman that we're not interested in being interviewed. Now, please see her off our property."

"Micah, I'm so glad to meet you. I'm Phoebe Jackson with the *Goshen News*."

The *Englisch* woman turned her attention toward him, and he tried not to squirm under her gaze. Her eyes were heavily made-up, and she had several earrings running up one ear. Her hair was cut in a short spiky style. Her lipstick reminded him of the pink taffy candy he'd loved as a child. She didn't look that much older than him.

"My editor sent me out here to ask a few questions about your Amish taxi business. Can you tell us how you got started?" She pushed the microphone in his direction and then glanced at a skinny guy, who looked to be about twenty and had terrible acne. "Charlie, you're rolling, right?"

"Uh-huh."

"So, Micah…"

Micah put out a hand and gently pushed her microphone down. Then he turned to the cameraman. "Charlie, stop rolling."

"But…"

"Stop, please."

Charlie looked at Phoebe, who nodded once—curtly.

"*Danki.* Now, if you'd be so kind as to leave my grandparents' property." He stepped off the porch toward their van, and Phoebe followed as if they were tied together by some invisible string.

"But this is a big story, a human interest story. People want to know how you got started."

"They can take a ride in my buggy and ask me then."

"You're from Maine, right?"

"How did you know—"

"Do they have Amish taxi drivers there?" Phoebe had once again pushed the microphone in his direction. "I couldn't find anything on the internet."

Micah stared pointedly at the microphone until she took the hint and dropped it. "In general it's difficult to find Amish businesses online since we don't own computers."

"But…"

"Look, Phoebe, I appreciate that you need stories to fill your paper."

"It's called the news for a reason." She trudged back toward her van as she stuffed her microphone, notepad and pen into a large shoulder bag—eyebrows drawn together, pink lips in a pouty frown.

Micah sighed and followed her. "I know that you're only doing your job, but my grandparents are very private and very old-fashioned."

"And what about you?"

"What about me?"

"Are you private and old-fashioned, too?"

Micah shrugged. "A little of both, I suppose."

Charlie had loaded his camera in the van. Phoebe opened the door, tossed her shoulder bag inside and then turned to give Micah a once-over. "Not too private to submit a selfie to our paper and win fifty dollars."

Micah shook his head. "I can explain that."

"What's to explain?" She hopped in the van and slammed the door shut, then rolled down the window. "Seems to me that if you're being paid for it, then you have no trouble being in the paper."

"I didn't submit that photo, and I'm sorry if I've offended you in some way."

"Oh, I'm not offended." She checked her lipstick in

the mirror, dabbed at the corner of her mouth and looked again at Micah as she slipped dark sunglasses on. "I'm a reporter, Micah. I will get my story. In this instance, I'll just have to interview your customers since you're not willing to go on the record."

"On the record? What do you think this is…a television show?"

"So you know about those, too." She tapped a finger adorned with bright pink polish against her lips. "Are you sure that you're really Amish?"

Micah felt his temper spike, but for perhaps the first time in his life, he brought it under control.

Phoebe reached into her bag, pulled out a business card and held it out the window until he took it from her hand.

"If you change your mind, give me a call."

And then they were gone.

Micah stood there, watching the red taillights disappear down the lane and trying to figure out how he was going to explain this to his *daddi*.

Chapter Ten

As May gave way to June, Susannah and Micah settled into a pattern of sorts. He would come in the morning to help her *dat* with the horses. Before he left, he'd stop by her quilting room, and they would make plans for the evening or the weekend or whenever they could find time to be together. It was becoming increasingly more difficult because his taxi business was doing so well, or at least that was the only reason she could think of that would cause him to be out every evening. He was no doubt running *Englischers* around until sundown.

He didn't share the particulars of his business with her, but she could well imagine that by the time he returned the buggy, walked home and ate the cold dinner waiting on the stove, it was too late for them to see each other.

Susannah assured him that she understood, though he was looking increasingly exhausted. Dark circles had formed under his eyes, and it looked to her like he'd lost weight. When she asked him about it, he only said, "I have a plan, Susannah."

"Care to share it with me?"

"I do." He glanced at the watch he'd begun wearing. "But not yet. Not now, when I'm rushed. We need to talk soon, but when we're not in a hurry or distracted."

He was certainly both of those things. She shrugged as if *soon* was fine with her. "But how do your grandparents feel about your long hours?"

"I don't know. *Daddi* barely speaks to me. He probably hasn't said a dozen words since he smashed my phone with his work boot."

"And your *mammi*?"

"She seems preoccupied. He doesn't seem well, and I think she's worried about him. For reasons I can't fathom, he refuses to talk about it."

"Should he go to a doctor?"

"Maybe. She's suggested it, but he won't even consider seeing a doctor. The last time she suggested it, he glowered at her and said, 'Does it look like I'm bleeding, Abigail?'"

"I could ask my *dat* to go over and—"

"I don't think that's a *gut* idea. At least not yet. But *danki*." He pulled her to her feet and into his arms, lowered his head to hers and inhaled deeply. "I sure am glad you offered to be my buddy when I came to town."

"Is that what I am to you?" Her voice was teasing, but Susannah knew that he heard the seriousness behind her question. They had kissed on several occasions since her visit with Dr. Kelly, and she was trying to let things unfold naturally and at their own pace. Some days that was easier than others.

"Yes…" His lips found hers, and for a moment, she forgot what she'd asked.

Then she pulled away. "I'm not sure it's appropriate for buddies to be kissing."

"Is that so?"

"Maybe."

"I guess we need to change your title, then."

"And what would we change it to?"

Micah rubbed at his chin as if he couldn't think of the word. Then he snapped his fingers. "I've got it. Girlfriend. You'll be the girlfriend, and I'll be the boyfriend."

Susannah rolled her eyes and turned back to her cutting table.

"My boyfriend should get going then, or you're going to be late for your first taxi client."

He walked up behind her, slipped his hands around her waist and lowered his voice. "I have a plan."

"You do?"

"Yup. And if it works, and I think it will, then I will have plenty of financial resources. I won't be at the mercy of my parents or my grandparents. And then you and I will sit down and decide what happens next."

She pivoted in his arms, looked in his eyes and marveled that she'd managed to fall in love with someone she was hoping wouldn't stay in Goshen more than a few weeks.

For the next three hours she focused on the quilt on her design table. She was working on a patchwork-star quilt the librarian had hired her to make for her soon-to-arrive grandbaby. Unfortunately she was having trouble focusing. Her thoughts insisted on wandering back over Micah's words.

What plan? What did he mean when he said *if it works*? And what was he thinking when he said they'd have to decide what happens next?

Was he hinting about marriage?

Was she foolish to jump to that conclusion?

And why hadn't she just asked him?

The questions tumbled through her head, but she soon pushed them away and immersed herself in the process of choosing fabrics, cutting squares and meticulously sewing them together. As for Micah, whatever his plan was, time would tell. He'd share the details with her when he was ready to. Until then she'd pray for patience, and that whatever he was cooking up was firmly in line with their *Ordnung*. The last thing they needed was another run-in with his grandfather.

Susannah woke to pounding on the front door and then the murmur of voices downstairs. She grabbed her robe and hurried to the living room, arriving in time to see Micah's grandmother leaving. "What is it? What's wrong?"

Her father had already returned to his bedroom, presumably to dress, since all of the lanterns seemed to be on.

"*Mamm*, what's wrong?"

"It's Micah." Her mother pulled her over to the couch. "He's been arrested."

"Arrested?"

"He's at the Goshen Police Department now. Abigail came and asked your *dat* to go down to the police station and see if he could work out the misunderstanding."

"What misunderstanding? Why did they arrest him?"

"It seems there's been a robbery."

"What?"

"And Micah was in the vicinity. The police pulled him in for questioning and decided to book him."

"Can they do that?"

"Apparently."

Her *dat* walked into the room, kissed her *mamm* on the head, then did the same to Susannah. "Try to sleep, and if you can't sleep, then pray."

And then he was gone, leaving Susannah wondering what had happened and what, if anything, she could do about it.

Micah looked up when he heard Thomas's voice. He couldn't hear what was being said. When no one appeared in the hall that led to the cells, he finally moved back over to his cot and sat down.

He stared down at his ink-stained fingertips. The photographing and fingerprinting seemed to have happened days ago. He became convinced this nightmare of an evening would never end. Once his initial fear had subsided, a sort of numbness had settled over him. It was almost as if he was standing a few feet apart from himself—watching the arrest, booking and jailing happen to someone else.

He'd never been in an *Englisch* jail. It was both better and worse than he'd imagined.

Better because he wasn't forced to share it with any petty criminals—the Goshen municipal jail allowed each person their own four-by-six concrete space. The stories of motorcycle gangs and hardened criminals roughing up the innocent Amish boy melted away into the night. No doubt, these stories were told to *youngies* to keep them on the straight and narrow.

And that was the worst of it. He'd finally committed his life to the straight and narrow, and look where it had landed him.

He heard footsteps and glanced up to see Susannah's *dat*.

"How are you, son?"

"I've been better. Did you come to get me out?"

"I came to try, but the officers are claiming they have video evidence."

"That I robbed the general store? That's not possible, because I didn't do it."

"Gut. Gut." Thomas reached into his pocket, pulled out an old pipe and stared at it a moment. Stuffing it back into his pocket, he glanced up at Micah and smiled. "My *dat* used to say the truth will out."

"The truth will out?"

"Ya."

"What does that even mean?"

"That given enough time, the truth will work its way out. If you didn't do this thing—"

"I didn't."

"Then you have nothing to worry about."

Micah looked around his cell—the small bed, the toilet and sink. It was all so humiliating. He turned his attention back to Thomas.

"Ya, I know. Just think, though. You're in good Biblical company."

"I am?"

"Paul and Silas spent time in jail."

"Oh, I suppose I remember that now that you mention it."

"Joseph, Samson, Jeremiah, Daniel, John the Baptist…"

"I didn't remember those, though I doubt they were in jail because someone thought they'd knocked over a general store."

"I would like to pray with you. Would that be all right?"

"Ya." Micah sighed and walked toward the bars separating them. "I could use some prayers right now."

He never expected to fall asleep, but he woke to someone in an adjacent cell complaining about instant eggs, and the guard telling him that this wasn't the Ritz. Whatever that was. He washed up at the sink, pulled the single cover up on his thin mattress and sat on the bed. Within a few minutes, a tray of runny eggs, cold toast and what had to be imitation bacon was delivered to his cell.

"Probably not what you're used to at home," the officer said. He almost sounded like he cared. The tag on his uniform said Officer Wright. The expression on his face said that he'd seen it all, and he probably had.

"Nein. It's not."

"Hopefully you won't be here long enough to get used to the food."

Micah cleaned his plate because he was starving. His restlessness grew as he realized that he was missing his taxi appointments. No doubt everyone had heard by now, though. He'd be lucky if anyone trusted him enough to ride in his buggy.

His heart felt as if it dropped somewhere close to the floor when he realized Susannah would have heard, as well. He wished he could get a message to her. She wouldn't believe him capable of doing such a thing. Susannah was a fair person. She wouldn't turn her back on him. Thinking of her made him feel better, and knowing he would see her again helped him to resist falling into a state of despair.

An hour later he was sitting in an interview room, Thomas next to him on one side of the table and two officers sitting across from them. One was in uniform and the other was in regular *Englisch* clothes.

"For the record, this interview is being recorded." The man in *Englisch* clothes straightened the sheets of paper in his folder. "Please state your name."

"Micah Fisher."

The man nodded toward Thomas, who tapped a finger against the table, smiled and said, "Thomas Beiler."

"And are you related to Mr. Fisher?"

"*Nein*, I'm his bishop."

"I'm Detective Cummings and this is Officer Decker. This interview is occurring at 9:35 on the morning of June 10." Cummings was tall and thin with red hair that had been recently buzzed. Decker was a woman in her forties and had yet to smile. "Mr. Fisher, please confirm that you've been read your rights."

"As officers were slapping the handcuffs on my wrists."

"A simple yes or no will do."

"Yes, I have."

"You are being held on suspicion of breaking and entering of the general store."

"Which I didn't do."

"We'd like to go over your statement, and then we'll talk about what happens next."

"What happens next is you let me go. I did not rob the general store."

Thomas's hand on his shoulder caused Micah to shut his mouth, which he supposed was the good bishop's purpose for being there. He took a deep breath and scrubbed his hand over his face. If ever there was a time he needed patience, it was now. And he needed it fast!

"Understandably Micah is upset." Thomas's voice

was quiet and his tone neutral. It worked to calm Micah down. "I'm happy to vouch for him. He's a *gut* worker, and he has never been in trouble before."

"We'll get to that. Again, just to confirm, Mr. Fisher, you waive your right to an attorney?"

"Yes."

Thomas nodded in agreement. "As I'm sure you know, we prefer not to become entangled in legal matters. Our goal is to remain separate and yet be *gut* members of the community."

"Yet you are entangled." Decker sat back, crossed her arms and waited until she was sure she had everyone's attention. "I've been on this police force for twenty-two years, and I appreciate and respect your culture. But you know as well as I do, Bishop, that we've had our share of Amish teenagers step over the line."

"And we've always cooperated and done everything in our power to compensate anyone for damages and see that the youth received counseling as needed."

"We're not talking about underage kids drinking beer behind the Dairy Queen. We have video evidence of this young man robbing the general store last night."

"That's not possible, because I wasn't at the general store."

"All right." Cummings tapped a pen against his pad of paper. "Give us your alibi, then. We'll verify it and we can have you out of here in time for lunch."

"My alibi?"

"Tell us where you were and who you were with."

Micah opened his mouth and then shut it. "I can't do that."

"Why?"

"Because I can't."

Susannah's father tilted his head toward Micah and lowered his voice, though, of course, the detective and office could still hear what he said. "It would be in your best interest if you would—"

"I can't, Thomas. I just…can't."

"All right. We seem to be at an impasse here. Micah, for whatever reason, can't tell us where he was, but if I understand *Englisch* law correctly, he doesn't have to prove his innocence. You have to prove his guilt."

Detective Cummings nodded at Decker, who pointed to a television on the wall and then hit some buttons on her cell phone. At first, the video was dark, showing little except for the front of the general store.

"This was taken from the store across the street twelve minutes before the alarm went off in the general store."

As they watched, a horse pulling an Amish buggy stopped in front of the general store. A young man stepped out, though the camera was too far away and the scene was too dark to tell who it was. The man was approximately Micah's height and build.

Decker paused the video. "Now, is there something you want to tell us?"

"*Nein*, because that's not me."

As they watched, the young man pulled out a crow-bar, busted the lock on the front door and hurried inside. They couldn't see in the store or what was happening, but suddenly the wail of a siren could be heard on the video.

"That was activated by the alarm attached to the cash register," Cummings explained. "The owner disabled the security alarm to the front door because it kept going off at random moments, but he left the one on the cash register drawer."

The time meter at the bottom of the video continued

to roll forward. Not long after the alarm went off, the Amish person ran out of the store, jumped into the buggy and drove off. Decker stopped the video and looked at Cummings, who focused on Micah.

"Son, it goes better for everyone if you just confess to what you did. Plead guilty, and I will personally speak with the judge and request the minimum sentence."

"I am not your son, and I wasn't the person in the video."

Cummings sat back with a sigh, as if it pained him greatly to hear Micah's words. Not even looking at Decker, he motioned for her to keep going. She pushed more buttons on her phone and another video came up, this time showing the opposite side of the buggy. The buggy had paused at a road crossing, directly underneath a streetlamp.

"A business on the next block has CCTV."

"What is that?"

"Closed-circuit television—it's a security measure so they can record any activity in or around the store when it's closed. We were able to pull this video and establish that it occurred in the same time frame as the first video, but it gives us a different point of view."

"So?"

Officer Decker looked at him for just a moment, as if he might be the dumbest person she'd ever encountered. Thomas had gone completely still, his eyes focused on the video. With a sinking feeling in his stomach, Micah turned his attention to it. He watched as the buggy came into view and then proceeded past the camera's field. Decker pushed more buttons on the phone; the horse and buggy moved backward. She then paused the video and zoomed in.

The first thing Micah saw was the scraped paint on the front fender. He'd asked Widow Miller about fixing it when he'd first started using her buggy. Her answer had been "Why? It travels the same whether the paint is perfect or scraped."

The second thing he saw was the passenger-side window, and taped to it was the sign that he had placed there, which read Amish Taxi.

He didn't know what Thomas said to the detective or what the detective said to him after that. His mind was spinning, and it was as if he couldn't process anything else.

It wasn't until he was back in his cell, until he heard the bars clank shut and the lock turn, that he managed to bring his attention back to the present.

Officer Wright had apparently escorted him back. Now Wright was studying him with a resigned look. "Guess you'll have time to get used to the food after all."

"What do you mean?"

"Do you have the money to post bail?"

"Nein."

"Neither does your bishop, apparently."

"So?"

"So that means you're staying until the judge is in court again, which will be two more days. Might as well make yourself comfortable." Officer Wright stepped closer to the bars, and something about his demeanor or the look in his eyes reminded Micah of the old men in Maine who sat around and told stories of the early days there. Something in his eyes spoke of experience and wisdom. Whatever it was, it caused Micah to listen— to really listen.

"I don't know what you did or why you did it. The

why doesn't matter so much at this point, and I can guarantee you that Judge Johnson isn't interested in whether you were mistreated as a child or are suffering depression. Johnson's an old-fashioned kind of judge. You do the deed, you pay for it."

"And what if I didn't do it?"

"Then you need an alibi, because from what I heard, they've got you on this one from three different directions."

Micah didn't answer. He was thinking about the buggy and the Amish man and the sign on the window.

"All I'm saying is that this place is not so bad. Food's terrible and you don't have TV or a library, but it's not that bad. But where you're going? It's not where a young man like you should spend a year or two. Do yourself a favor and wise up before the judge gets here."

And with those words of comfort, Micah found himself once again alone.

Susannah couldn't believe it. She tried to process what her *dat* told her. She could tell he wasn't holding anything back, but she couldn't believe what he was saying. There was no way that Micah was guilty of breaking into the general store.

She tried to speak to his grandparents. John Fisher took one look at her and headed to the barn. Abigail stepped out on the porch, but the conversation went nowhere.

"I know you love your grandson."

"Of course I do, but Micah has never seen the world as the rest of us see it."

"You're saying you believe he did this?"

"I'm saying he might have convinced himself it was

okay. I don't know. Sometimes what a person is capable of will surprise you."

"Have you been to see him?"

His *mammi* shook her head once, and that was the end of the conversation. She turned and walked back into the house, leaving Susannah standing there and wondering what to do next.

Visiting Deborah didn't go much better.

"He didn't do this, Deborah. I know he didn't."

Deborah held up her hands in surrender. "I don't want to believe it, either."

"He didn't do it."

"You said he's been out late a lot."

"So what?"

"So four other stores have been robbed in the last two weeks."

"What? And you think he did that? You think Micah was traveling up and down Goshen knocking over stores? Why would he even do such a thing?"

"You're the one who said that he has a plan. Didn't he say if it worked, he would have financial resources?"

"Which could mean a lot of other things besides robbery."

Deborah stopped separating dollar bills in the cash drawer of her family's vegetable stand. She walked around the table and put her arms around Susannah, who had determined she would not cry. She was not going to cry about Micah, because he did not do this.

"Have you tried to see him?"

"I have." She brushed her sleeves across her eyes.

"And?"

"He saw me the first time—that was yesterday. Told

me that he didn't do this, and that he would be out by the weekend, so I should have the fishing poles ready."

"Maybe he will. Maybe he is innocent. I'm just so sorry you're going through this."

"Then he asked me not to come back."

Deborah stepped back, hands still on Susannah's shoulders, as if she needed to get a better look at her best friend's face. "Why would he say that?"

"Because he said that without an alibi…" The tears resumed streaming down her face. "Without an alibi, they just might pin this on him, and there wasn't anything he could, or would, do about it."

"All right. So we know where to start."

"What do you mean?"

"I mean, you're going to see him again this afternoon. Didn't you say the judge is in court tomorrow?"

"Yes."

"So go to him today. Go now. It's important that you see him before he appears before the judge."

"What am I supposed to do? What am I supposed to say?"

"You're going to convince him to explain where he was and who he was with."

Chapter Eleven

Micah didn't look up when he heard the guard open the outer door. Whoever was in the cell at the end of the hall had a large family. They'd all come to see him. He couldn't hear much of what they said, but what he did hear was like a knife in his gut.

"We know you didn't do this."

"We're going to get you out."

"Dad's working on the bail money."

"Mom knows a guy who knows a guy who's a lawyer."

Whoever that person was had a very engaged family—a family who believed in his innocence. Micah didn't know if the person was guilty or innocent, but he did know that he was a lucky man to have so many people on his side.

Only two people had come to visit Micah.

His bishop.

And his girlfriend.

He hadn't seen or heard from his grandparents.

He'd used his one phone call for the bishop, so he hadn't spoken to his parents, and he wasn't sure he wanted to. What could he tell them? How could he explain this situation that threatened to change the course of the rest of his life?

And then the scent of rose lotion pulled him away from his dark thoughts.

If anything, Susannah looked prettier than the day he'd seen her standing by the mailbox with Sharon and Shiloh. She wore a light blue frock and a white apron and, of course, the ever-present white *kapp*.

"Why are you smiling?"

"Just remembering the first time I saw you without that *kapp* on."

"Five minutes," Officer Wright said. He offered to bring Susannah a chair, but she shook her head no and thanked him.

"Why did you come back?"

"Because I needed to see you." She pulled in her bottom lip, and he knew that she was fighting back tears, which caused his defenses to crumble.

He stared at the ceiling, and when he looked at her again, he'd regained control of his emotions. It wasn't that he was afraid of crying in front of her. He wasn't one of those guys who believed that men shouldn't ever show their emotions. It was more that he felt if he let go of the reins that were holding them in, he might never regain control again.

"Things were going too well," he whispered.

"What things?"

He only shook his head.

"Come over here."

Micah could hear the trembling in her voice, and it nearly undid him. He closed his eyes for a moment, but when he opened them she was still there.

"If you are going to do this to yourself, to us, then you owe me this much. Come over here and look me in the eye."

"I can't tell you where I was. I—"

"You can't tell the judge. I know. You said that before. But if you can't tell me the when or where, then you can at least tell me the why."

So he stood and walked to where she was waiting. They weren't supposed to touch. The poster on the wall proclaimed that rule loud and clear. But then Micah had never been good at following the rules. Susannah's hands were wrapped around the cell's bars. He ever so gently wrapped his hands around hers, figuring they had one minute, maybe two, before one of the officers came busting through reminding them to stand three feet apart.

"Tell me why." Her voice was soft, and when he looked in her eyes he saw a whole world of hurt.

But he also saw something else… He knew that she trusted him or at least she wanted to.

"I can't tell you where I was…"

The rattle of keys at the end of the hall told him the officer was coming through.

"I can't tell because I promised I wouldn't. I gave my word, Susannah. And what kind of man would I be if I couldn't keep my word? You deserve better than that."

She swiped at her eyes. "Okay."

"Okay?"

"*Ya.* Okay."

The officer separated them before either could say anything more, but what Micah saw before she walked away almost sent him to his knees because it wasn't judgment or disappointment or anger—it was love.

Micah stood in a type of waiting room next to his court-appointed lawyer. The man was definitely under thirty years old, and he looked as if he'd slept as little as Micah had. When Micah had refused to give an alibi, he'd only asked, "You're sure?" When Micah confirmed that he was very sure, the man—Rafael Rodriguez—had grinned and said, "Chances are you're going away to prison, but we're going to make them earn it."

He opened the door, and they walked into the main courtroom.

The judge had apparently been working for several hours already. He glanced at the clock, as if he was wondering whether he could take a lunch break. The man was in charge, wasn't he? Couldn't he just order the court adjourned? Or perhaps Micah was remembering the single court scene he'd watched on television wrong.

Judge Johnson was older, white haired, and Micah could tell in a second that he did not suffer fools.

The bailiff called Micah's case, and he and Rafael walked forward to stand before the judge.

It was a moment that Micah understood he wouldn't forget if he lived to be a hundred. It was surreal, standing there before a man who had the power to free or imprison him. There was a spiritual lesson here that wasn't lost on him—the power of forgiveness and the sacrifice of Christ standing before the one and true God. He'd heard it preached often, but at that moment, he felt it clean through to his soul.

"Mr. Rodriguez, does your client still refuse to provide an alibi?"

"He does."

"Mr. Fisher, you are charged with aggravated burglary." Rafael had explained that *aggravated* meant he had a weapon—in this case, a crowbar that could be seen in the video and was used to break the lock on the front door. "How do you plead?"

"I plead not guilty, Your Honor."

Rafael had told him what to say word for word. They'd even practiced.

"I assume you still have no means to post bail."

"That's correct, Your Honor."

"Then I have no choice but to remand you to the Elkhart County Jail until…" He must have consulted a calendar, because he picked up some half-glasses, perched them on his nose and stared down at something. "Looks like it'll be July 18 before you can have a jury of your peers."

He took the glasses off and looked at Micah—really looked at him—for the first time.

"Mr. Fisher, you're certain that you want to remain behind bars until that time?"

"I don't see as I have a choice, Your Honor."

"You most certainly do. If you can prove that you weren't the person in the video…"

"Objection, Your Honor. The accused is not required to prove his innocence, but rather—"

"I know the law, Mr. Rodriguez." Johnson shook his head as if he needed to rid himself of a pesky fly. "I've seen the video, and I have to say that the evidence here is strong. Strong enough to hold Mr. Fisher over for a trial."

"You can't know that's him."

"That will have to be proved at the trial. Until then…" He raised his gavel to strike it against the desk when someone spoke up from the back of the room.

"I can provide Micah with an alibi."

Relief washed over Micah in that moment because he knew that voice. His legs felt suddenly wobbly and his hands shook so that he had to clasp them together.

Rodriguez stepped closer and said, "Steady there. Don't faint on me, Fisher."

But Micah understood what Rafael Rodriguez and Judge Johnson couldn't—what they would very soon know. Micah understood that this nightmare was over, and that he'd be able to go home.

Thomas walked on one side of him, Susannah on the other, as Micah left the Goshen Municipal Jail.

"How about we have some lunch before we go home?" Thomas nodded at a coffee shop across the street.

Susannah squeezed his hand. "We heard the food wasn't so good in there."

"You heard right. I'm starved."

They ordered hamburgers, fries and shakes before they got down to business.

"Levi Hochstettler?" Susannah was sitting across from him. No doubt she wanted to be able to look into his eyes while he explained the last few weeks. "You were with Levi? I wasn't aware you even knew him."

After thanking the waitress for the shakes she left on their table, Thomas asked, "And why was that so hard to admit?"

"The first time I picked up Levi for a ride, he had me drop him at this old barn over on the east side of town. It was an *Englischer*'s place, from the look of it."

"What was he doing there?"

"Rebuilding the engine on a 1956 Mercedes."

"Levi always was *gut* with small engines," Thomas said.

Susannah leaned forward. "And you helped him?"

"Not at first, but after the third ride, he figured he could trust me." Micah had already consumed half of his shake. He didn't realize how bad jail food was until he was a free man and eating good food again. "I did some engine repair up in Maine, so I offered to lend a hand. This was last week, the same week that my business first got off the ground."

"This is why you've been so tired."

"I knew I was stretching it—burning the candle at both ends as the old folks say—but it seemed like too good an opportunity to pass up."

Thomas grunted, but he didn't interrupt.

"So I was helping Thomas in the morning, running my buggy service in the afternoon and helping Levi at night. We were about halfway through with the rebuild…"

"And then?" Susannah was twirling her *kapp* string, completely engrossed in his story.

"Then Levi found a buyer. An *Englisch* guy who was willing to pay top dollar."

"Which was, no doubt, a lot of money."

"It was, and the *Englischer* put down a deposit, so we knew he was good for it. But the problem was that he needed it for some race this weekend."

"A race?"

"Some race with old cars. They give you a map at the last minute. I didn't really understand that part."

"The Great American Race." Thomas smiled when they both turned to stare at him. "I'm a bishop, but I'm still a man. This race has been around since the eighties."

The waitress brought their food, and for the next few minutes, no one spoke as Micah made up for lost calories. When he finally pushed back his plate, Susannah and her father shared a smile.

"Don't say it, *Dat*."

"Growing boy needs his food."

They all laughed, and it felt good. Micah wanted to

pull Susannah into his arms. He wanted to thank her for standing by him, but he understood that doing so in the middle of a burger joint in front of her father probably wasn't a great idea.

"So the *Englischer* needed the car fast. He was willing to pay good money and Levi was willing to share what he made." Susannah shook her head. "What are you not saying?"

"Levi's parents." The bishop ran his fingers through his beard.

"Exactly." Micah took up the story. "Levi's parents are quite strict. They were already unhappy that he was working on car engines."

"I've talked to them about that," Thomas said. "Levi is good with his hands, good at fixing things. If he'd been born *Englisch*, there's no doubt he would have been an engineer of some sort. It seemed to me that allowing him to use those talents in a way that was acceptable would solve the problem."

"But it didn't?" Susannah had pushed her plate away and was again leaning forward, no doubt ready to pull the rest of the story out of him.

"I'm only sharing this because Levi told me as we left the courtroom that I should tell you everything." He glanced at Susannah but directed the next part to the bishop. "He's thinking of leaving the faith. Well, not leaving exactly. He has an *onkel* who is Mennonite and has a shop in Ohio. Says he can give Levi all the work he needs. But he insisted that if Levi really wanted to do it, then he would have to save the money for the bus fare as well as a deposit on a place to live. They have eight young ones, so there's no room at their house."

"But if he could sell the Mercedes…"

"Then he'd have enough money to go." Micah finally pushed away his plate. "He's going to come and talk to you tomorrow."

Thomas nodded as if that settled things.

"Okay." Susannah held up her left hand and began counting off points. "You were helping Levi. He was sharing the profits with you. You were definitely not in Widow Miller's buggy, and you did not rob the store…"

"I never doubted that," Thomas said.

"Why couldn't you just explain that to the judge?"

"Because I promised Levi I wouldn't tell. I gave him my word that I would not be the one to tell his parents. He wanted to do it, in his own way, in his own time."

"You didn't want him to get in trouble? You were willing to go to jail for that?"

Micah didn't answer right away. When he looked at Susannah and Thomas, at these two people who had come to mean so much to him, he knew that he could be completely honest.

"I've been on the outside most of my life. I'm not really sure why. Rebellious nature that needs taming, or maybe…maybe I hadn't met the right person who could settle me down." He paused and looked directly at Susannah—smiled and resumed his story. "I know what it's like to walk a tightrope at home, and how important it is to have one person who you can trust with your real self, with who you really are. You two have been that for me, and I have been that for Levi. It was important for me to honor that commitment."

"When Levi stood up for you in court, when he provided your alibi, he also put himself on the line with his parents."

"Exactly."

"You know, Micah. The one thing that you can give and still keep is your word. It seems to me that you showed maturity and wisdom today."

Which seemed to settle the matter as far as Susannah and Thomas were concerned. Micah didn't know what would happen when he went home to his grandparents.

And he certainly didn't know who had stolen Widow Miller's buggy and broken into the general store, but he did know that it wasn't him, and that it was time to do what Levi was doing. It was time to stand up and be true to who he was. He would probably never be a traditional Amish person, but he loved his faith and he had the support of the bishop for his Amish buggy service. If that wasn't good enough for his grandparents, then perhaps it was time he accepted he was bound to disappoint some of the people who meant the most to him.

Their disappointment might hurt, but it wouldn't change who he was.

Micah stared at his *daddi* in disbelief. "You can't make me do that."

"You're right. I can't. However, I can issue an ultimatum."

"An ultimatum?"

"*Ya*, for sure and certain."

"That's not… It's not how we do things."

"How would *you* know?" His *daddi*'s voice rose like a wave crashing over them. "How would *you* know how we do things? You've spent the last three days in an *Englisch* jail."

"For something that I didn't do."

"You have only one foot in our world. The other is firmly planted in the *Englisch*."

"That's your opinion."

"*Nein*, son. It's a fact, and I will not stand for it any longer."

Micah glanced at his *mammi*. Was that sympathy he saw in her eyes? Perhaps, and yet she didn't jump to his defense.

"You will inform Thomas of your decision to join the church on Sunday morning."

"I haven't made that decision yet."

"You will inform him on Sunday or before Sunday, or you will find another place to live—perhaps one of your *Englisch* friends will take you in."

His *daddi* pushed himself up from the table with his one good arm, and that was when Micah noticed that his hand was shaking. He shifted his left shoulder, as if it pained him. Micah had the sudden realization that his *daddi* was not a young man, that he was aging. He felt a stirring of sympathy for him, which was immediately wiped away by the man's next words.

"I've given you time, Micah. We all have."

"And I have done what you asked."

"You think this life is a game of some sort—a long procession of parties and reckless decisions and stepping back and forth across the line that our community has plainly drawn to keep us separate." He reached for his hat and crammed it on his head. "That is your choice, but I won't abide it a moment longer. We've all coddled you much too long. It's time for you to make a decision. Choose the life you wish to live."

And with that final declaration he stormed out the back door.

Neither Micah nor his *mammi* moved. Finally, she sighed and stood, beginning to clear away the dishes.

"Tell me you don't agree with him."

"Doesn't matter if I do or not."

"It matters to me."

Mammi placed the dishes into the sink and stood there for a moment, staring out the window. When she turned back toward Micah, he saw such conflicting emotions in her eyes that it tore at his heart.

Was this really all his fault?

Was he tearing his family apart? The memory of his last week at home in Maine threatened to rise, but he quickly pushed it down. They'd understood him little more than his grandparents.

Instead of lecturing, *Mammi* walked over to where he sat, pulled a chair up close and sat so that their knees were touching. She reached for his hand and stared down at it a moment. When she finally raised her eyes to his, Micah's heart sank.

She was on his *daddi*'s side.

He knew what was coming.

"Your *daddi* isn't wrong, not in his intent. Perhaps his presentation could use a little work." She attempted to smile, but it slid away. "He loves you, Micah. We all do. However, you are twenty-five years old. You're a man, not a *youngie*."

"I know that." His throat was suddenly tight. He had to push the words out. "I know I'm not a child."

"And yet you so often act like one."

Coming from his *daddi*, the words would have stung. But the words were whispered by his *mammi*, and the look she gave him? It held only compassion.

"He's feeling older these days. The mornings are hard because he wakes so stiff, and then some mornings, like today, the indigestion bothers him."

"I'm sorry he isn't feeling well, but it gives him no right…"

"It gives him every right. He doesn't complain, and I'm not telling you this so you'll feel sorry for him. Though, of course, you should have sympathy for others, especially your family. I'm telling you this so you'll understand."

She ran a wrinkled finger under his suspender, straightening it, and patted his shoulder lightly. "What your *daddi* understands, which you don't, is that this life is but a fleeting matter, like a passing mist. You think that you have all the time in the world to decide the course of your life, but none of us has an unlimited amount of time to make our choices. Today is the day for you to make your decision."

She patted his shoulder again, then pushed herself into a standing position. That was when Micah knew that all was lost. She would not intervene on his behalf.

He felt numb all over.

Why did it seem that everyone was against him?

First that foolishness about the break-ins, as if he would do such a thing. And now this.

His *daddi* was actually going to force him to join the church. He'd actually been considering doing so, but now… To have it dictated to him put a sour taste in his mouth. He couldn't make a decision like that because someone said he must. It would be a lie.

The one thing you can give and still keep is your word.

Thomas's words came back to him like an arrow to the heart. When he made a decision to join the church, he was giving his word, so he needed to be certain. Didn't he?

And what was the alternative?

Or did he even have one?

Chapter Twelve

He spent that afternoon and the next morning in a bit of a fog. He saw Susannah when he stopped by her *dat*'s farrier shop, but he didn't speak to her of what was happening with his grandparents. He wasn't ready. What if she agreed with them?

There was little work for him in the shop, so he took off early and headed to town to hopefully pick up some Saturday passengers in his buggy service. He lasted less than an hour. After he took one Amish girl to the wrong store, and an *Englisch* woman asked why they were traveling in a circle around the same block, he knew his mind wasn't on his work. Apologizing, he dropped her off where they'd started—free of charge.

He simply couldn't focus.

The anger and sense of unfairness grew until he thought that he might explode. He picked up his Amish-taxi sign and made his way back across town, returning the horse and buggy to Widow Miller's and making his way to his grandparents' house. There he paced back and forth in the barn for the better part of a half hour.

Only ten thirty in the morning, and yet it felt like the

day had lasted forever. He walked inside, looked around and headed back out. He was barely aware that he'd grabbed his hat from the mudroom, and he didn't realize he was walking toward Susannah's until he caught sight of her playing outside with her little *schweschdern*. Sharon and Shiloh spied him at the same moment and dashed toward him.

"We found a grass snake in the garden." Sharon grabbed one of his hands. "We placed rocks around him so that we can watch what he does."

"He can't get away," Shiloh added, standing close and worrying one hand inside the other. "I was scared at first, but Susannah says it won't hurt us."

He followed them to the edge of the garden. The grass snake was only a few inches long and bright green. He'd probably been sunning himself when the girls had noticed him and quickly built a perimeter—one that the snake would have no trouble sliding over or through, but Micah didn't bother telling them that.

"I'm going to get him some grass." Sharon bounded off toward the edge of the garden.

"Susannah said he eats frogs. I'm going to see if I can find one." Shiloh dashed toward the water trough they used to irrigate the garden.

"Watch out for snakes," Susannah called from her place at the north end of the garden.

"Too late for that advice." Micah plopped down on the ground beside her.

She rolled her eyes. When he didn't say anything else and only sat there brooding—that was the only word for it—she bumped her shoulder against his.

"What's wrong? Did your favorite baseball team lose last night?"

"*Nein.*"

"I thought you'd be in a fine mood today, since you're no longer considered the bandit of Goshen."

"And yet I'm still the black sheep." The unfairness of it seemed to press down on him. Why couldn't people simply accept him like he was? Why couldn't he be Amish without following every one of their silly rules? Why were rules even necessary?

"Something has happened." Instead of pushing him, Susannah waited, which was something she was very good at.

It was one of the things he appreciated about her. While his mind dashed back and forth, her steady presence helped to calm him down. He stared at the garden for several minutes—a part of his mind hearing the girls giggling over the snake, a part of his mind still back in his grandparents' kitchen.

Finally, he blew out a noisy breath and told her everything.

Susannah wasn't exactly shocked at what Micah told her. She'd suspected such a thing might happen sooner rather than later, but she was disappointed that it had happened the morning after he'd been proved innocent of the break-ins.

"I'm a little surprised you're taking it so hard."

Micah jumped to his feet and began to pace back and forth. "Taking it hard? I'm about to be thrown out on my own."

"Just last week you were talking about having a plan and not being dependent on your grandparents anymore."

"But I need more time. I'm not… I'm not ready yet."

When she smiled at him, he collapsed on the ground

beside her. "Maybe I should have seen this coming. I'm not sure, to tell you the truth."

"It seems to me that your grandparents are simply forcing the issue—an issue that you were already thinking about."

"They're saying I have to decide between being Amish or *Englisch*. That I have to decide now."

"They're saying if you're going to stay in their home, you have to decide now. No one can force you to make the decision to join the church, Micah. You can take as long as you need, but the process of deciding... Well, it must be hard on them."

He flopped onto his back and shielded his eyes against the sun. "I know you're not on their side. You've stood by me through all the ups and downs since I've been here. You even visited me at the jail."

"Twice."

He stole a peek at her and made a valiant effort to keep the perturbed expression on his face. "Twice," he conceded.

"You've had a difficult week. I definitely think you deserve a break."

He pulled up a handful of grass and tossed it at her, and Susannah couldn't help smiling. He had changed so much from the young man she'd seen step out of an *Englischer*'s truck in downtown Goshen. He had stepped into adulthood when he'd begun his own business, when he'd begun planning for the future, and certainly when he'd put his integrity over his freedom.

But the playful Micah lurked underneath, and maybe that was okay, too. Many adults were too serious. She loved that he was able to lighten her mood with a touch or a smile or a silly suggestion. Amish Taxi? She couldn't believe he'd come up with that. She was beginning to think of him as her Amish rebel. And rebels weren't such bad things—they kept everyone on their toes, weighing their decisions rather than following blindly along.

Still, she understood that it was hard to leave the carefree years of *rumspringa* behind, to embrace being an adult and accept responsibility for all of one's actions. Her cancer had forced that role upon her earlier than most, and something in Micah's upbringing had allowed him to put off any such change again and again. Perhaps it was because he was the only son in a family full of daughters. Perhaps it was simply his personality.

Regardless, she rather agreed with his grandparents that it was time for him to decide. They could have suggested such a thing a bit more tactfully, but John Fisher had never been known for his tact.

"You refuse to cut me any slack," Micah muttered.

"Is that what you want?"

"*Nein.* I like that you're honest with me."

She shrugged and the look he shot her caused the heat to rise in her cheeks. Just like that, the subject of remaining Amish was behind them, and the playful Micah was back.

"You worry me when you get that look in your eyes."

Sharon picked that moment to dump two handfuls of grass onto Micah's stomach. He launched himself off the ground, chasing her around the garden until she fell into Susannah's lap squealing and laughing. Shiloh had plopped down cross-legged beside them and rested her head in the palm of her hand.

"I think we should take our snake to the pond."

"Do you, now?" Susannah reached out to tug on her *kapp* strings.

"Actually, that's not a bad idea." Micah sat up straighter. "But I've heard that what snakes really like is rivers—especially grass snakes, because…you know, there's lots of grass growing on the banks of the river."

Susannah tried to catch his eye, but he was avoiding looking directly at her. "I don't like where you're going with this."

"It's Saturday. What else do you have to do?"

"I'm supposed to be minding Sharon and Shiloh while our parents are visiting church members."

"And you will mind them at the river."

Which, of course, started a chorus of "Please" and "Can we?" and "We promise to be good."

"No fair," she laughed. "It's three against one."

"I'll even help you pack a lunch." Micah pulled her to her feet, stepped close enough to scoot her *kapp* strings back over her shoulder. "Maybe we can wear these two out, and they'll take a nap."

"I hate naps," Shiloh murmured.

"We're too old for naps!" Sharon jumped from one foot to another. "Oh, I know. I'm going to get a box to put Simon the Slippery Snake in."

She dashed off toward the house in search of a box. Shiloh stood clasping her hands and watching Susannah. "Are we going? I think Simon would like the river better than our garden. If you think it's okay."

It was probably the look on Shiloh's face that made up Susannah's mind. She was such a sweet, serious girl—maybe too serious. A few hours at the river would do them all good.

"All right, but we need to be back well before dinner. I promised *Mamm* I would have food on the table by five. Besides, it's supposed to rain."

Micah waved away any concern. "A summer shower can't stop us from having fun."

Twenty minutes later, Susannah had changed the girls into older dresses, Micah had helped to pack the makings for a picnic lunch and they were traipsing across the field to the back of her parents' property. She'd left a note telling her *mamm* where they were going.

The clouds had begun building toward the west.

"Weather's changing." Susannah pointed the fishing rods she was carrying toward the darkening sky. Shiloh and Sharon were walking in front of them—Sharon carrying the box with the snake, Shiloh carrying an old quilt they would use to spread across the ground.

"Still a long ways off. We'll be fine, Susannah." Micah shifted the picnic basket to his right hand and slipped his left arm around her shoulder. His fingers trailing her neck caused goose bumps to cascade down her arm. She deftly stepped to the left, out of his embrace.

Micah laughed. His melancholy mood over the argument with his *daddi* seemed to have passed. She'd learned that was both a strength and a weakness of Micah's. He had the ability to move past things in a way that she envied. She tended to dwell on things too long.

But he also moved on without ever attempting to resolve the problem. She knew from experience that such a course was akin to kicking the can down the road. It only postponed what needed to be done, and many times that indecision had a ripple effect, causing even worse problems and more difficult decisions.

But now wasn't the time to tell Micah that, if it was even her place to do so.

He was laughing, assuring her that a little rain

wouldn't hurt them and predicting they would catch enough fish to feed her entire family.

They crossed one field, then another. The path to the river that they used skirted around and then behind an abandoned barn. She hadn't been in that thing in years. Her *dat* kept saying he was going to tear it down, but looking at it now, she felt a rush of affection for the thing. It seemed to be leaning gently—its boards weathered to a soft gray, and she realized she enjoyed seeing it there. The old barn was a symbol of permanency, a fond memory from her childhood. She'd played in it many a summer as a young girl.

She led her way around it, then down the path that led to a lower pasture and the river. Perhaps Micah was right. Maybe it was the perfect day for a picnic.

Micah felt in his element walking toward the river at the back of the Beiler property. Perhaps the argument with his *daddi* wasn't as bad as he'd feared. Oh, he understood his *daddi* was serious, but as Susannah had pointed out…he'd been thinking of moving into town anyway. That had been part of his big plan—independence and hopefully a chance to live his own life.

It wasn't that he didn't want to be Amish.

But why was everyone pushing him to choose such a narrow path so soon? The day before, he'd been in the Goshen jail. Didn't he deserve a day or two of rest? Why couldn't they just enjoy a Saturday fishing on the river?

Well, the answer was: they could.

They spent the next hour setting up their picnic area, releasing Simon the Slippery Snake and helping the girls put the fishing lines in the water. The sun was now obscured by the clouds, and a westerly wind had picked up.

"Perfect day for a picnic," he murmured, lying back on the blanket with his hat over his eyes.

"Not exactly."

"You're sweet, Susannah, but I don't think you'll melt in the rain."

"Perhaps we should start toward the house."

He tipped his hat back enough to peer at her. "Seriously? We just got here."

"The storm seems to be coming in sooner than they predicted. I wouldn't want to get caught."

"Can you stop worrying for a few minutes?"

The words came out sharper than he'd intended, and he could tell that he'd hurt her feelings by the way she pulled in a breath and sat up suddenly—her posture ramrod straight.

"Don't do that."

"Do what?"

"Get your feelings hurt because I have a big mouth."

"Oh, do you, now?"

"We both know I do." He found her hand and entwined his fingers with hers. He glanced at the girls, still standing with their backs to them, staring at their fishing line. Could he sneak in a kiss before they turned around? Because Susannah suddenly looked quite kissable.

Susannah's voice dropped. "I do realize that I tend to be a bit too serious. You're not the first one to suggest such a thing."

"I didn't mean anything by it. Only that I wish you could relax."

"You mean you want me to be more like you?"

"Yes! Exactly. Then there would be two of us renegades in the Goshen Amish world."

When she laughed, Micah knew he was forgiven.

"Perhaps we should eat before this storm soaks everything."

Micah's stomach gurgled, and he realized he'd not eaten breakfast. He'd been too busy worrying over his *daddi*'s ultimatum. He helped her to make peanut butter and jelly sandwiches, then convinced the girls to leave their poles resting on the bank.

"What if we catch a big one?" Sharon was jerking her pole up and down in the water. "I want to be here to pull him out."

"I promise to run and catch him if some whale starts to pull your pole into the water."

Which caused Sharon to laugh. They joined Shiloh and Susannah on the blanket and the next hour was spent enjoying the food while playing a game of I Spy. It was only when he noticed Susannah attempting to hold down the corners of the blanket that he noticed the wind had picked up quite a bit.

"I truly think we should go back." Susannah began loading the leftover food back into the basket, the wind tugging at her *kapp* and her skirt and the edges of the blanket.

It was in that moment that the weather abruptly changed.

"It stopped, Susannah." Sharon clapped her hands. "The wind stopped. So we can stay. Right? Please…"

But suddenly Micah wasn't thinking about fishing or picnics or even finding a private moment to kiss Susannah. He jumped to his feet and strode away from the picnic, away from the trees, where he could have a better view of the sky.

The edges of the storm had turned an ominous olive green. He checked the tops of the trees again, as if to confirm what the back of his brain was telling him. Maine only averaged two tornadoes a year, but he vividly remembered 2017, which had been one of their worst years in terms of weather. An unusually high number of tornadoes—seven in all—had touched down that year, one within sight of his parents' farm.

He knew the signs.

A green sky.

Sudden drop of wind.

Unnatural stillness.

And then he saw it, dipping down from the western sky.

"We need to go." He ran back toward the picnic, grabbed Shiloh in one arm and Sharon in the other. "Leave that, Susannah. We need to go now."

And then they were running across the field and toward the abandoned barn.

Chapter Thirteen

Susannah saw Micah running toward them, hollering at her, though she couldn't make out his words. He'd picked up the girls and was urging her to do something. She put her fingers to her ears, attempting to yawn and pop them, and that was when she heard the freight train bearing down on them.

Then he'd run back and was shouting in her ear, "We need to go."

She dropped the basket and ran with him. How was he able to carry both girls? She'd tried to pick Shiloh up just that morning, to set her on a chair and tie her shoes. They'd laughed that she'd staggered under her *schweschder*'s weight.

They were halfway across the lower field, Micah leading the way, still holding both of her *schweschdern*. Susannah stumbled, dropped to the ground, and that was when she looked back. The funnel cloud seemed to be nearly on top of them. She sat there on the ground, gawking at it, frozen.

The noise was tremendous.

The sight was terrifying.

She barely realized that Micah had once again turned back and was squatting beside her and yelling something. It was the sight of Shiloh and Sharon that brought her back to her senses. Both girls were wide-eyed, their arms wrapped around each other, tears streaming down their faces.

Susannah jumped to her feet.

"The barn," she screamed.

And then they were running, Micah again carrying Sharon and Shiloh. He didn't put them down until they'd reached the barn door. He struggled against the wind to pull it open, and Susannah thought, *This is it. We're going to die here because the door is stuck.*

Her heart cried out to God then. It wasn't so much a prayer, not words that she would later remember. It was the cry of her heart—for Shiloh and Sharon and Micah and, yes, for herself, as well. Because she realized in that moment that she wanted to live. Her fear of cancer and the uncertainties of life were whisked away and she felt an actual pain in her heart.

She wasn't ready yet.

She didn't want this to be it.

She wanted to live and embrace life and see her *schweschdern* grow into fine young women with families of their own.

The door didn't open so much as it flew out of Micah's hands, and then they were tumbling inside.

Susannah didn't know if it had been a good or bad idea to shelter in the decrepit barn, but there wasn't time to second-guess herself, and there wasn't anywhere else to go. Her eyes met Micah's for a brief second, and she saw there the same fear and yearning and love that she was feeling.

But before she could process anything, before she could attempt to speak or reassure Shiloh and Sharon, Micah knocked them all to the ground. He threw himself on top of the three of them, and then the noise seemed to become an entity unto itself—roaring and crashing and colliding. And the structure—the barn that she had such fond memories of—simply broke apart.

She must have passed out.

She gradually became aware of Micah shaking her. She opened her eyes to find his tearstained face close to hers.

"You're alive."

"*Ya*, I think so."

She attempted to sit up. The world seemed to tilt, and she dropped her head into her hands. "I think I'm going to..."

And then she vomited up everything she'd eaten sitting on the old patchwork quilt as the girls fished in the river.

The girls...

She jerked upright, and a tremendous weight shifted from her head to her heart.

Sharon sat beside Shiloh, crying and holding her *schweschder*'s hand. Shiloh's arm was twisted at an awkward angle, but it was the blood running down her face that caused Susannah to gasp.

She didn't run so much as crawl over to Shiloh's side.

"She's still breathing." Micah squatted beside her. "I tried... I tried to stop the bleeding." It was then she noticed he'd taken off his shirt, compressed it into a bandage and placed it against Shiloh's head. "Her arm, it's broken, but it's the cut on her head that I'm worried about."

Susannah glanced up at the roof, but it was gone. Instead of the storm they'd fled, she saw clouds broken here and there by blue sky.

"How long…"

"Fifteen minutes. I've been trying to wake you. I didn't want to leave them."

"Go. Go now."

"Are you…"

"I'm fine, Micah. Go and get help for Shiloh."

Susannah didn't watch him leave. Her attention was completely focused on Shiloh and Sharon. Shiloh had yet to move or open her eyes. Sharon was crying so hard that she'd begun to hiccup. Susannah pulled the young girl into a hug.

"She's going to be okay, Sharon. Micah has gone for help."

"I was so…so… I was so scared."

"We all were."

"Uh-uh." She wiped the back of her hand across her eyes. "You weren't scared. You stood up and ran, just like Micah. But I was so scared that Micah had to… He had to carry me. And now Shiloh is… Shiloh is dead."

She broke down into sobs. Susannah put a hand on top of her head. She'd somehow lost her *kapp*, and her hair was a tangled mess, but none of that mattered. "Micah didn't carry you because you were too scared to run."

"He didn't?"

"*Nein*. He carried you because his legs are longer, so he can move faster."

"He saved us."

"*Ya*. He did." Susannah took Sharon's hand, opened her small palm and placed it gently on Shiloh's chest. "Can you feel her breathing?"

"Uh-huh."

"She's going to be okay."

"But she's bleeding."

"Something must have hit her on the head. She's going to need stitches, and she'll probably have a big head-ache."

"She will?"

"Ya."

"Her arm looks funny. What's wrong with her arm, Susannah?"

"It's broken."

"Broken?"

"The doctors can fix that, Sharon."

"Micah went to get help?"

"He did."

"What can we do?"

"We can pray. Do you want to do that with me?"

Sharon had been crouching on her knees. Now she plopped onto her bottom, placed her palms together and squeezed her eyes shut. Together, they began to pray.

A part of Micah's mind noted the destruction that he ran through. A line of fencing, gone. The chicken coop to the side of the garden was now sitting in the middle of the lane. He skidded to a stop at the garden, where they had all been sitting just hours ago. It looked as if the ground had been freshly tilled. Every plant, every seedling, every tomato post had simply vanished.

Which was when he glanced up at the house and saw that the side of it facing the garden had no wall at all. He could peer inside, like an *Englisch* dollhouse he'd once seen in a store. He craned his neck back, stared up at the second floor and into Susannah's room.

What if she'd been there?

What if they'd all been there?

The question paralyzed him for a few seconds, until sirens began to echo through the air.

How many had been hurt?

Were his grandparents all right?

And how was he going to get help to Shiloh?

He sprinted to the east pasture. Percy, the buggy horse, was gone—of course he was. Susannah's parents had taken him to visit church members. He put his hands on his knees, attempting to draw in deep breaths, and when he glanced up he saw it—Susannah's bicycle leaning against the side of the barn.

Micah jumped on it and sped off down the lane.

Later he wouldn't remember bicycling the two miles or dashing into the phone booth. He didn't recall picking up the phone, dialing 911 or dropping the receiver.

The ride back to the old barn was a blur.

All he knew for certain was that he had to get back to Susannah. He had to be there with her and he needed to help with the girls.

He pumped the pedals of the bicycle, sailing back down the road, turning into the lane, jumping off when he reached the yard and sprinting back across the field, back to the old barn.

He skidded to a stop in the doorway of the barn, though there was no longer a door. There weren't even walls so much as there were piles of debris. The roof was gone completely, the windows blown out, glass glittering on the ground.

What if the glass had blown in?

What if the entire thing had collapsed on them?

He understood in that moment that he would never

forget what he saw when he stepped into the main room of the barn. Susannah was holding Shiloh in her lap. The head wound had bled through the shirt he'd pressed against her head. Shiloh raised eyes that were dazed, that seemed not to see him, but then she smiled, and the fear that had seized his heart melted away.

"Micah, I hurt my head."

"And her arm. Her arm is all wrong." Sharon darted toward him, snagged his hand and pulled him across the room—toward Shiloh and Susannah.

He knelt beside them, and that was when Susannah raised her eyes to his. When she reached out and touched his face, the tears that he'd been holding back, that had been strangling his voice and blurring his vision, began to flow freely.

Micah didn't know how long they sat there, huddled together. He was suddenly aware of the sound of a vehicle approaching and the blip of a siren. He kissed Susannah on top of the head, squeezed Shiloh's hand and said to Sharon, "Let's go tell them where we are."

By the time they stepped out of the barn, two paramedics were jogging across the field, carrying a child's gurney and a medical box. They'd left their vehicle on the side of the road. Micah could just make out the strobe of its red lights.

It wasn't until they'd placed a splint on Shiloh's arm, put a clean compress on her head and were loading her into the back of the ambulance that Micah thought to ask, "Are there more injured?"

"We've had a lot of calls, but so far no fatalities."

Micah put a hand on the back door of the ambulance to keep the paramedic from shutting it. Sticking his head inside, he assured Susannah, "I'll stay with Sharon. We'll find your parents and tell them. We'll all be right behind you."

Susannah seemed about to say something, but instead she nodded her head and turned her attention back to Shiloh.

And then the door was slammed shut, the ambulance was pulling away and Micah was left standing on the side of the road, Sharon's hand clutching his.

Susannah knew her way around a hospital. She'd spent enough time in one when she'd gone through her cancer diagnosis and treatment. She understood the reason for the X-rays that the doctor insisted on taking. She wasn't bothered by the IV they started in Shiloh's arm or the fact that they had to shave a swath of hair to clean the wound and stitch it up.

"Now our hair will match," she assured her *schweschder*, which earned her a smile.

She was able to explain the machines that beeped, noting Shiloh's heart rate, blood pressure, oxygen saturation, respiration and temperature.

"What does it all mean, Susannah?"

"It means you're going to be okay. Are you feeling better?"

"I didn't like that needle."

"*Ya*, needles are no fun."

"And now I'm so—" she paused for a huge yawn "—sleepy."

"Close your eyes and rest."

"But…"

"I'm not going anywhere."

"You'll wake me when *Mamm* and *Dat* get here?"

"If you want me to."

"I want you to."

Shiloh's right arm was still in a splint. She turned onto her left side, placed her hand under her cheek and closed her eyes. She was asleep before the clock on the wall had ticked off another minute.

A thousand questions crashed through Susannah's mind.

Was their house okay?

Had anyone else been hurt?

What about Percy and the chickens and the barn cats?

What about her neighbors?

For the first time in her life, she wished that she had an *Englisch* phone so that she could know what was happening. But then she realized she didn't need to know. *Gotte* knew. *Gotte* was in charge, just as He had been when He'd watched over them. She didn't need to know every detail this minute. She only needed to trust Him.

So she did what she'd done in the barn with Sharon. She prayed—for her parents, her neighbors, for Micah and Percy and her *freinden*. She prayed for the doctors and nurses. She prayed that the break in Shiloh's arm wouldn't be too painful.

By the time the doctor came in—a young woman sporting a name tag that read Dr. Emir—Susannah felt calmer and ready for whatever news the doctor brought. She was petite with long black hair pulled back in a simple ponytail holder and large owlish glasses.

After introducing herself and confirming that Susannah was Shiloh's relative, Dr. Emir said, "Your sister was very lucky. The head wound wasn't too terribly deep, and the arm was a fairly clean break."

"So both will heal quickly?"

"It's amazing just how fast young ones heal. If it was

you or me, it would take a while, but Shiloh shouldn't have any trouble at all. We'll need to cast her arm, of course."

"Her favorite color is purple."

Dr. Emir smiled. "I'll see what I can do."

Then the doctor cocked her head and asked, "Are you sure you're okay? I can have someone look at…" She raised a hand to her own face, and that was when Susannah remembered that she'd been cut from some of the debris.

"Oh, I think it's fine."

"Best to clean it up anyway. You wouldn't want infection to set in. You're going to have your hands full taking care of your *schweschder*." And that—the doctor's use of their word—eased Susannah's heart more than she could explain. They were Amish and *Englisch*; of course they were. But they were also one community that pulled together in times of trouble.

As the doctor turned to go, Susannah asked, "Have you heard anything else? About injuries, or…" She couldn't bring herself to say the word *deaths*.

"The emergency room has been pretty busy. They're saying it was an F2 and that it left a pretty wide swath of destruction. Fortunately most of it was farmland."

Susannah nodded. She wondered how long it would be until her parents arrived and whether Micah was still with Sharon. And then her mind slipped to the realization she'd had as they ran toward the barn—that she loved Micah, that he was the person she wanted to spend the rest of her life with.

Today wasn't the time to tell him that, to explain to him how she felt, but wasn't that what she'd learned in that moment of terror when the tornado dropped out of the sky?

Life was precious, and it was best to take nothing for granted.

As a nurse stepped into the room and cleaned her wounds, Susannah promised herself that she would hold that lesson close to her heart and in the front of her mind.

She'd spent too long caught in the past. Starting this moment, she would plant her feet firmly in the present.

Chapter Fourteen

Micah wasn't sure if he should stay and wait for Susannah's parents or go check on his grandparents. Based on what he could see, the tornado had veered off in the opposite direction. He was sitting on the front porch steps with Sharon when Susannah's parents pulled up in front of the house.

Sharon flew into her mother's arms.

Micah tried to explain what had happened. He'd reached the part where the ambulance had arrived and picked up Susannah and Shiloh, when Thomas interrupted him. "Get in. You can tell us the rest on the way to the hospital."

"I should check on my grandparents."

"Of course. We'll drop you off."

"*Nein.* Go. Go to the girls, and tell them both I'll be there as soon as I can."

He realized as they pulled away that neither of Susannah's parents had commented on the destruction of their home.

Homes could be rebuilt.

Their one concern had been for their daughters.

He was thinking of that as he crossed back toward his grandparents' farm. It was the people in your life that mattered, not the things. It didn't at all matter what he wore, or whether he owned a phone, or if he drove a buggy or a car. What mattered was how you treated the people you cared about, and he realized with sudden clarity that he had not treated his grandparents well.

In fact, he'd taken them for granted—eating their food, staying in their home, allowing his *mammi* to wash his clothes and his *daddi* to provide his transportation. It was true that he'd given them money, but had he given them his respect and his gratitude? In truth, he'd thought they owed it to him, but no one really owed anyone else anything. It was their love for him that had provided for his needs.

And what had he done in return?

He'd mocked their way of life.

Shown a complete lack of respect for their years of hard work.

Argued at every possible turn.

He'd been a child, as surely as Sharon and Shiloh were children. When he'd realized that it was up to him to get Sharon and Shiloh and Susannah to safety, he'd left that side of himself behind in the path of the tornado. The storm had done more than threaten their very lives, it had pushed Micah into the world of being an adult—of being responsible for someone else and embracing that responsibility.

There would be no turning back.

He let out a breath he didn't realize he'd been holding when he saw his grandparents' house. It was completely intact, without so much as a tree limb littering the yard.

He took the front porch steps two at a time.

His grandparents were in the living room—*Mammi*

sitting next to *Daddi* on the couch, holding a glass of water and pressing it to his lips. As for his grandfather, his face was an ashen gray and his breathing seemed labored.

"What happened?"

"We heard the…the tornado. John figured you went over to Susannah's. He was going to check on you when he collapsed on the front lawn. I managed to get him inside."

"*Daddi?* Can you hear me?"

His grandfather opened his eyes, though he seemed to have trouble focusing. His breathing was ragged, and though it wasn't hot at all in the house, sweat ran in rivulets down the side of his face.

"I shouldn't…shouldn't have said…"

"Not now, *Daddi*." Micah clasped his hand. "It's forgiven and forgotten. Now, we need to get some help."

He sprinted out of the room, to the barn where he kept the replacement phone he'd purchased. He only hoped it was charged. Had he even used it since he'd arrived home from jail? He pulled it from the shelf where they kept miscellaneous tools, powered it on and ran out into the yard.

Two bars and 8 percent power.

It should be enough. It would have to be.

For the second time that day, he tapped in the number 911.

The person who answered took down the information, told him what to do and insisted on staying on the line until the paramedics arrived.

He found the bottle of aspirin in his *mammi*'s medicine cabinet. After Micah had given one to his *daddi*, the emergency dispatcher walked Micah through checking his pulse, which was weak but steady.

"It's important that you keep your grandfather calm. We have an ambulance on the way to you right now."

Five minutes passed, then ten, and then finally he heard the scream of the siren coming down their lane. He wasn't too surprised when the two paramedics who hopped out of the vehicle were the same ones he'd seen earlier.

"Busy day for you," the woman said, patting him on the shoulder before rushing past him and into the house.

They stabilized his grandfather and loaded him into the ambulance.

His *mammi* looked a bit dazed. "You can go with them, Mammi."

"I can?"

"I'll bring the buggy."

"*Danki*, Micah." She pulled him into a hug, clung to him fiercely for the space of three heartbeats and then she, too, was gone.

Micah wanted nothing more than to hitch up the buggy and tear out after them.

But what would his *daddi* want him to do?

After all, he would only be waiting and pacing at the hospital. They wouldn't even let him in the room for the first hour or so. Instead of rushing off, he walked through the living room and into the kitchen. He found a pot of red beans cooking on the stove, so he turned the gas burner off. He covered the pot with the lid and pushed it to the back of the stove. The clock above the sink said that it was nearly five in the afternoon, when his *daddi* always looked after the animals.

So Micah did those chores, too.

Finally, he walked into his grandparents' room to see if there was anything there that they might need.

His grandmother's purse and sweater were hanging on a hook near the door. He grabbed both and had turned to go when he spied her worn Bible on a nightstand. Picking it up, he ran a hand over the cover. The corners were worn and the letters on the front were barely discernible.

Sinking down onto their bed, he opened the book and stared at the inscription.

To Abigail, the love of my life.
John
October 15, 1978

His *daddi* had been a young man then, younger than Micah was now if he'd done the math correctly. And yet he'd known that Abigail was the woman he wanted to spend his life with. He hadn't questioned his love for her or her love for him. And look at them now. They'd survived the terrible accident that had taken his arm, raised a houseful of children and now they were helping to raise Micah.

He realized in that moment how much he respected his *daddi*. Micah might not always agree with his opinion on things, but he admired how he'd spent his entire life caring for and providing for his family. He recalled the look on both of their faces as *Mammi* had sat beside him holding the cup of water. There was simply no doubt how much they loved each other.

Micah wanted that.

He wanted that kind of consistency in his life.

He wanted someone who looked at him like his *mammi* looked at his *daddi*.

And he was absolutely certain he knew who that someone was.

* * *

Susannah had moved to the waiting room and was sitting with Deborah by the time Micah found her. He explained about his grandfather—the doctors had assured him that his condition was stable, but that he didn't need more visitors at the moment. "How's Shiloh?"

"*Mamm*'s in with her now, and *Dat*'s taken Sharon to get something to eat and then outside to check on the horse."

"What about you?"

"What about me?"

"Have you eaten anything?"

"*Nein.*"

Micah reached for her hand, pulled her to her feet and then told Deborah where they were going. The room was virtually filled with *Englisch* and Amish. The latest reports were thirty-four people injured, but no fatalities. Three homes had been damaged—two Amish and one *Englisch*, though it sounded like Susannah's had taken the most direct hit.

"I'm sure I have something to eat in this bag." Deborah hoisted her large purse off the floor and onto her lap. "*Ya*. I have gum and peanut butter crackers and..."

Micah leaned down and said, "*Danki*, but I'm going to take Susannah to the cafeteria to get her some hot food."

Deborah raised her eyes to his, glanced at Susannah and then smiled. "*Gut* idea. You should do that. I'll just stay here, and if anyone is looking for you two, I'll tell them where you are."

"*Danki,*" Susannah said, enfolding her friend in her arms. She then left with Micah, tucking her hand in the crook of his elbow.

The cafeteria was staying open later than usual, owing

to the aftermath of the tornado. They both grabbed sandwiches and coffee, and Micah carried their tray to a table in the corner of the room.

Susannah took a couple of bites and then sat back, studying him instead of eating.

"You should finish that. You're going to need your energy. Your *schweschdern*, they can be a handful."

She could tell he meant it in a teasing way, that he was trying to lift her mood, but she wasn't ready for that yet.

"Micah, I need to thank you."

"*Nein*. You don't." He closed his eyes and rubbed his forehead with his fingertips. Finally, he pushed his tray away, crossed his arms on the table and focused on her. "I shouldn't have talked you into going to the river. I'm always doing that. Trying to find a way to goof off and dragging someone along with me, and today the result was that Shiloh was hurt. That's on me. That's my fault."

She could tell he was surprised when she reached across the table and covered his hands with hers. "I didn't see our house, but they told me. Half of it's gone. Is that right?"

"*Ya.*"

"So if we'd been home, if we hadn't gone to the river, there's at least a fifty-fifty chance we'd have died in that house today."

"Please don't say that." His voice was husky with emotion, and when he raised his eyes to hers, she saw tears sparkling there.

"You saved us, Micah, and I am grateful that you did. You saved your *daddi*, too. *Gotte* has used you today, and… I'm just glad that He brought you here."

Micah swiped at his eyes, then sat up straighter and squared his shoulders. "Are you saying that you'll go fishing with me again?"

"I could be talked into it."

She'd tried to match his light tone, but it was a facade that was simply too hard to keep up. He reached for her hands, pulled them to his lips and kissed them.

"I love you, Susannah Beiler."

"You do?"

"Tell me you haven't known that for some time."

"I hoped, but *nein*, I wasn't sure."

"I let you teach me how to sew."

"You're not very good at it."

"Susannah, I'd be interested in alpacas if it meant I could spend more time with you."

"I don't have any alpacas."

"Not my point."

They sat there another ten minutes, until they became aware that others needed their table. Susannah wanted to tell him how she felt, but how was she supposed to do that in the middle of the crowded cafeteria? Then they were walking down the hall, and Micah stopped abruptly. He glanced left, then right and then pulled her into an alcove, wrapped his arms around her and held her close.

"I was so frightened," he admitted.

"Me, too."

"And when I realized…" He framed her face with his hands and kissed her softly on the lips. "When I realized that I might lose you, I understood how important you are to me. I knew when I saw that tornado dipping out of the sky that I would do anything for you, for your family, for us."

He kissed her again, then thumbed away the tears slipping down her face.

"I love you, too," she whispered.

"You do?"

"Don't act surprised."

"I thought you were dating me to keep your friends safe."

"That was the original plan."

He kissed once more, and she felt safe again. No longer worried about what might fall out of the sky. He kissed her, and she knew that somehow everything was going to be all right. Then he pulled her back out into the hall. Together they walked toward the waiting room, knowing that whatever news they faced, they would weather it together.

Shiloh was released from the hospital the next morning.

Micah's grandfather stayed an additional three nights, and then was only allowed to go home when he promised to rest and stay off his feet. They'd put in a stent to clear up a blockage in his main artery, and the doctor had started him on a statin medication.

Micah was in the room when the cardiologist had said, "You've had a heart attack, Mr. Fisher. As we discussed, that means your heart is damaged. You're going to need to give yourself a few weeks to build your strength back up, and I expect you to be in my office in seven days for a follow-up."

Once they were home, his *daddi* insisted on sitting on the front porch while Micah unharnessed and cared for the horse. When Micah had checked everything and closed up the barn, he climbed the steps to find his *daddi* still there. The sun was dipping toward the horizon, and through the window Micah could see his *mammi* heating one of the casseroles a neighbor had left.

"I'd like to talk to you, Micah."

Instead of arguing, as he might have the week before, Micah sat in the adjacent rocker and waited.

"I meant what I said when you found me the day of

the tornado. I shouldn't have spoken to you as I did that morning. I shouldn't have tried to force your path."

"You care about me."

"I do, but I see now that your path is different from mine. Doesn't mean it's wrong."

Micah fought to hide his surprise. When his *daddi* caught his eye and smiled, Micah admitted, "You're not the only one who needs to apologize. I see now that I've been bullheaded out of habit and immature because I could be."

A red bird landed in front of them in the yard, hopping back and forth as it pecked at the dirt.

"I'm going to ask Susannah to marry me."

"She'll make a fine *fraa*."

"Not yet, though. I won't ask yet. I want to give her time to recover."

His *daddi* sighed, then pushed himself up and out of the rocker. "If there's one thing I've learned, it's never assume you have more time."

Micah understood what his *daddi* was saying, but he also appreciated what Susannah had been through. He didn't want to take anything for granted, least of all her. He also wanted to be sensitive to her feelings.

Three days later, Detective Cummings stopped by to say they'd found the person who had burglarized the general store as well as quite a few others. "Not an Amish kid. He thought that by acting like one, by looking like one, he could get away with it."

"And he almost did."

"His mistake was stealing Widow Miller's buggy twice. She saw him driving out of her place, and she walked to the phone shack."

"Good thing it's across the road."

"She called the police, and we caught him as he drove into town."

Which seemed to end the matter as far as Micah was concerned.

Two weeks later, a workday was held at the Beiler place. They began before the sun came up, and by the time it was setting, a new home had been framed. They'd been staying in a *dawdi haus* over on the Hochstettler place, and Micah knew they'd be glad to move back home.

Each day of the next week, Micah went over in the afternoons to help finish the house. Each time he arrived, a different group of men were nailing up Sheetrock or painting rooms or finishing the porch. By the end of June the house was completed. They'd opted for a one-story design, since Susannah's parents didn't see themselves having any more children.

Micah tried to stay away, but he found he couldn't.

He was drawn to the Beiler place. It felt like home to him. He needed to be there.

He arrived after dinner, their first dinner in their new home. Shiloh and Sharon insisted on showing him their new room. "We have window seats," they squealed, then insisted he sit there while they brought him a pillow, blanket, three books and two dolls.

Susannah stood in the doorway laughing.

It wasn't until the girls were in bed and Susannah's parents had moved to the front porch to enjoy the cool evening, that he asked her to go for a walk. And it was there at the pasture fence, under a covering of stars, that Micah asked Susannah to marry him.

"You're sure?" She reached up and touched his face. Micah wanted to memorize the way that her fingers felt against his skin. More than that, he wanted her this close to him every day for the rest of his life.

"I've never been so sure of anything."

"Even though…"

"You can't have children? *Ya.* I'm aware."

"That's a big thing, Micah."

"It's not as big as my love for you. Now, if you said you didn't love me, that would be a big thing."

"Of course I love you."

"Then you'll marry me?" He felt as if he'd laid his heart before her. He felt as if, with Susannah by his side, he could do anything.

"*Ya*, I'll marry you."

"*Gut.*" He kissed her once, then again, and then pulled her into his arms. "We can build here or on my *daddi*'s place."

"You've thought that far ahead?"

"I need to provide for my family."

"What about Maine?"

"It'll still be there, but I can't leave now. Not with *Daddi* needing help. I don't want to leave."

"I thought you couldn't wait to get back."

"Oh, I will go back. We'll go at least once a year, and who knows—maybe someday we will move there. But not now. We'll know when the time is right."

"But…"

His kiss stopped her protests. When he finally pulled back, he craned his head back and looked up at the stars. "See those, Susannah?"

"*Ya*, I see them."

"*Gotte* did that."

"Indeed, He did."

"And if He did that, He can also provide you and me

with a family. It might not be a traditional one—it could be adoption or fostering or simply kids who need a place to stay, whose families are struggling…"

"I hadn't thought of that." She snuggled in closer, pulled his arms around her and whispered, "But I'd like it. I'd like it very much."

To Micah their future seemed full of endless possibilities, like the stars that were endlessly stretched out above him. It didn't matter to him whether they ended up with a houseful of children or lived out their lives just the two of them. What mattered was that they'd found each other, that they'd been given a second chance.

It was one he didn't mean to squander.

* * * * *

If you loved this story,
pick up the other books in the
Indiana Amish Brides series,
A Widow's Hope
Amish Christmas Memories
A Perfect Amish Match
The Amish Christmas Matchmaker
from bestselling author
Vannetta Chapman.

Available now from Love Inspired!
Find more great reads at www.LoveInspired.com.

Dear Reader,

Have you ever felt defined by the things that have happened to you? It might be a disease or disability. It might be something from your past. It might be a mistake that you made.

Susannah Beiler has gone through cancer diagnosis and treatment. Now she is well, but she feels less than whole. She feels as if people see a cancer survivor instead of the woman she's become. More than that, she's afraid to dream or plan for the future. She tries to be happy in the present and grateful for what she's been given.

Micah Fisher has been coddled all his life. It's not his fault that he's the youngest sibling and only boy in a family of eight children. Life has taught him that it's okay to go with the flow, that each day is to be enjoyed. He doesn't understand the point of rules, and he wishes everyone would lighten up a little.

Susannah and Micah seem to be set on a collision course, but instead they develop a friendship—and eventually a love—that neither expected. Life can be like that sometimes—surprising. As for their future, God isn't finished with either of them yet, in the same way He isn't finished with you or with me.

I hope you enjoyed reading *An Unlikely Amish Match*. I welcome comments and letters at vannettachapman@gmail.com.

May we continue to "always give thanks to God the Father for everything, in the name of our Lord Jesus Christ" (*Ephesians* 5:20).

Blessings,
Vannetta

Clang, clang, clang.

The hammering outside her new schoolhouse grew
louder. Eva Coblentz moved to the window to locate
the source of the clatter. Across the road she saw a man
pounding on an ancient-looking piece of machinery with
steel wheels and a scoop-like nose on the front end.

When he had the sheet of metal shaped to fit the front
of the machine, he stood back to assess his work. He
knelt and hammered on the shovel-like nose three more
times. Satisfied, he gathered up his tools and started in
her direction.

She stepped back from the window. Was he coming to
the school? Why? Had he noticed her gawking? Perhaps
he only wanted to welcome the new teacher, although his
lack of a beard said he wasn't married.

She glanced around the room. Should she meet him
by the door? That seemed too eager. Her eyes settled on
the large desk at the front of the classroom. She should
look as if she was ready for the school year to start. A
professional attitude would put off any suggestion that
she was interested in meeting single men.

LIEXP0220

Eva hurried to the desk, pulled out the chair and sat down as the outside door opened. The chair tipped over backward, sending her flailing. Her head hit the wall with a painful thud as she slid to the floor. Stunned, she slowly opened her eyes to see the man leaning over the desk.

He had the most beautiful gray eyes she'd ever beheld. They were rimmed with thick, dark lashes in stark contrast to the mop of curly, dark red hair springing out from beneath his straw hat. Tiny sparks of light whirled around him.

"I'm Willis Gingrich. Local blacksmith." He squatted beside her. "Can you tell me your name?"

The warmth and strength of his hand on her skin sent a sizzle of awareness along her nerve endings. "I'm Eva Coblentz. I am the new teacher and I'm fine now."

Don't miss
The Amish Teacher's Dilemma
by USA TODAY *bestselling author Patricia Davids,*
available March 2020 wherever
Love Inspired books and ebooks are sold.

LoveInspired.com

LIEXP0220

Get 4 FREE REWARDS!

We'll send you 2 FREE Books plus 2 FREE Mystery Gifts.

Love Inspired books feature uplifting stories where faith helps guide you through life's challenges and discover the promise of a new beginning.

The Wrangler's Last Chance
JESSICA KELLER

Their Wander Canyon Wish
ALLIE PLEITER

FREE
Value Over
$20
